BY MAX BROOKS

NOVELS

Minecraft: The Island

The Zombie Survival Guide:
Complete Protection from the Living Dead

World War Z: An Oral History of the Zombie War

GRAPHIC NOVELS

The Zombie Survival Guide: Recorded Attacks

G.I. Joe: Hearts & Minds

The Extinction Parade

The Harlem Hellfighters

A More Perfect Union

© MOJANG

MINECRAFT™
THE ISLAND

MINECRAFT™
THE ISLAND

MAX BROOKS

CENTURY

1 3 5 7 9 10 8 6 4 2

Century
20 Vauxhall Bridge Road
London SW1V 2SA

Century is part of the Penguin Random House group of companies
whose addresses can be found at global.penguinrandomhouse.com.

Penguin
Random House
UK

Published in the United Kingdom by Century, an imprint
of Penguin Random House UK, London.

Published in the United States by Del Rey, an imprint of Random
House, a division of Penguin Random House LLC, New York.

www.penguin.co.uk

A CIP catalogue record for this book is available from the British Library.

HB ISBN 9781780897745
TPB ISBN 9781780897752

Book design by Elizabeth A. D. Eno

Printed and bound by Clays Ltd, St Ives Plc

Penguin Random House is committed to a sustainable future
for our business, our readers and our planet. This book is made
from Forest Stewardship Council® certified paper.

To Michelle and Henry,
who keep me from being
an island.

THE FOLLOWING IS BASED ON TRUE EVENTS.

INTRODUCTION

I wouldn't expect you to believe the world I'm about to describe, although your reading these words means you're already here. Maybe you've been in this world for a while but just discovered the island. Or maybe, like it was for me, the island is your introduction to this world. If you're alone, confused, and scared out of your mind, then you're exactly where I was on my first day. This world can seem like a maze and, sometimes, like a bully. But the truth is that it's a teacher and its trials are just lessons in disguise.

That's why I've left this book behind—so my journey can help you with yours.

©MOJANG

MINECRAFT™
THE ISLAND

CHAPTER 1

NEVER GIVE UP

Drowning!

I woke up underwater, *deep* underwater, and this was my first conscious thought. Cold. Dark. Where was the surface? I kicked in all directions, trying to find my way up. I twisted and turned, and then I saw it: a light. Dim, pale, and far away.

Instinctively I shot for it, and quickly noticed that the water around me was growing brighter. That had to be the surface, the sun.

But how could the sun be . . . square? I must be seeing things. Maybe some trick of the water.

Who cares! How much air do I have left? Just get to it. Swim!

My lungs ballooned, little bubbles escaping from my lips, racing me for the distant light. I kicked and clawed the water like a caged animal. Now I could see it, a ceiling of ripples coming closer with each desperate stroke. Closer, but still so far away. My body ached, my lungs burned.

Swim! SWIM!

Crack!

My body writhed as a sudden jolt of pain shot from toes to eyes. My mouth opened in a choked scream. I reached for the glow, grabbing for breath, for life.

I exploded into the cool, clean air.

I coughed. I choked. I wheezed. I laughed.

Breathing.

For a moment, I just savored the experience, closing my eyes and letting the sun warm my face. But when I opened my eyes, I couldn't believe them. The sun *was* square! I blinked hard. The clouds, too? Instead of round puffy cotton balls, these thin, rectangular objects floated lazily above me.

You're still seeing things, I thought. *You hit your head when you fell off the boat and now you're a little dazed.*

But did I fall off a boat? I couldn't remember. I couldn't remember anything, in fact; how I got here, or even where "here" was.

4

"Help me!" I shouted, scanning the horizon for a ship or a plane or even a speck of land. "Please, somebody! Anybody! HELP!" All I got was silence. All I could see was water and sky.

I was alone.

Almost.

Something splashed inches from my face, a flash of tentacles and a thick, black and grayish head.

I yelped, kicking backward. It looked like a squid, but square like everything else in this strange place. The tentacles turned to me, opening wide. I gazed right into a yawning red mouth ringed with white razor teeth.

"Get outta here!" I hollered. Mouth dry, heart pounding, I splashed clumsily away from the creature. I didn't have to. At that moment, the tentacles closed, blasting the squid in the other direction.

I floated there, frozen, treading water for a few seconds, until the animal disappeared into the deep. That's when I let out a long, throaty, tension-draining "ughhh."

I took another deep breath, then another, then a whole lot more. Finally, my heart settled down, my limbs stopped jerking, and, for the first time since I woke up, my brain switched on.

"Okay," I said aloud. "You're way out in a lake or ocean or whatever. No one's coming to save you, and you can't tread water forever."

I did a slow, 360-degree turn, hoping to see some thread of coastline I'd missed before. Nothing. In desperation I tried one last scan of the sky. No planes, not even a thin white trail. What sky doesn't have those trails? One with a square sun and rectangle clouds.

The clouds.

I noticed they were all moving steadily in one direction, away from the rising sun. Due west.

"As good as anywhere," I said, giving another deep sigh, and started swimming slowly west.

It wasn't much to go on, but I figured the wind might help me along a little bit, or at least wouldn't slow me down. And if I went north or south, the breeze might slowly blow me in an arc so I'd end up swimming in circles. I didn't know if that was really true. I still don't. I mean, c'mon, I'd just woken up, probably with some kind of massive head injury, at the bottom of an ocean, and was trying really, really hard not to end up back there.

Just keep going, I told myself. *Focus on what's ahead.* I began to notice how weird my "swimming" was; not the *stroke, pause, stroke* motion, but the sense of gliding across the water with my limbs along for the ride.

Head injury, I thought, trying not to imagine how serious that injury might be.

One good thing, I noticed, was that I didn't seem to be getting tired. Isn't swimming supposed to be exhausting? Don't your muscles burn and quit after a while? *Adrenaline,* I thought, and tried not to imagine that emergency gas tank running out.

But it would. Sooner or later, I'd lose steam, cramp up, go

from swimming to treading water, then from treading water to floating. Of course, I'd try to rest, bobbing up and down to conserve energy, but how long could I keep that up? How long before the cold of the water finally got to me? How long before, teeth chattering, body shivering, I finally sank back down into the darkness?

"Not yet!" I blurted out. "I'm not giving up yet!"

Shouting out loud was enough to perk me up. "Keep focused! Keep going!"

And I did. I kept swimming with all my might. I also tried to be über-aware of my surroundings. Hopefully I would spot the mast of a ship or the shadow of a helicopter, but at the very least, it would take my mind off my current predicament!

I noticed that the water was calm, and this gave me something to feel good about. No waves meant no resistance, which meant I could swim farther, right? I also noticed that the water was fresh, not salty, which meant that I had to be in a lake instead of an ocean, and lakes are smaller than oceans. Okay, a big lake is just as dangerous as an ocean, but c'mon, you got a problem with me trying to look on the bright side?

I also noticed that I could see the bottom. It was deep—don't get me wrong, you could sink a pretty decent office building and never see the top—but it wasn't bottomless like the ocean is supposed to be. I could also see it wasn't level. There were tons of little valleys and hills.

That was when, off to my right, I noticed that one of the hills had grown so tall that its top disappeared beyond the horizon. Did it break the surface? I turned north, northwest, I guess, and swam in a straight line for the hill.

And before I knew it, the hill grew into an underwater mountain. And a few seconds later, I actually thought I saw its top sprout above the water.

That's gotta be land, I thought, trying not to get my hopes up. *It could be a mirage though, a trick of the light or some mist or* . . .

That's when I saw the tree. At least I thought it was a tree, because, from that distance, all I could make out was a dark green angular mass perched atop a dark brown line.

Excitement propelled me like a torpedo. Eyes locked forward, I soon saw other trees dotting a tan beach. And then, suddenly, the green-brown slope of a hill.

"Land!" I shouted. "LAAAND!"

I'd made it! Warm, firm, solid ground! A few strokes and I'd be there. A wave of total relief washed over me . . . and just like a real wave it washed right back out.

I barely had a second to celebrate before the island came into full view. By the time I reached the shore, I was just as confused as the moment I'd woken up.

The island was square. Or, rather, it was made of squares. Everything: sand, dirt, rocks, even those things I first thought were trees. Everything was a combination of cubes. "Okay," I said, refusing to believe what I was seeing. "Just need a minute is all, just a minute." Standing in waist-high water, breathing, blinking, I waited for my eyes to clear. I was sure that any minute, all those harsh right angles would return to soft, curvy normalness.

They didn't.

"Gotta be that head wound," I said, wading ashore. "No problem. Just make sure you're not bleeding too bad and—"

Instinctively, my hand went up to find the supposed injury, and as it came up in front of my face, I gasped.

"Wha . . . ?" There was a fleshy cube at the end of my rectangular arm, a cube that wouldn't open no matter how hard I tried. "Where's my hand!?" I shouted, my voice rising in panic.

Head swimming, throat closing, I looked nervously down at the rest of me.

Brick-shaped feet, rectangular legs, a shoebox-shaped torso, all covered in painted-on clothes.

"What's wrong with me!?" I hollered to the empty beach.

"This isn't real!" I screamed, running back and forth, trying to tear the painted clothes off my body.

Hyperventilating, I rushed back to the water, desperate for the calming reflection of my face. Nothing greeted me. "Where am I?" I shouted to the shimmering sea. "What is this place?"

I thought of the water, of how I'd woken up . . . but had I?

"This is a dream!" I said, relief breaking into my panicked voice, reaching for the only thing I could think of. "Of course!" And for a second I almost pulled myself together. "Just a crazy dream, and soon you'll wake up and . . ."

And what? I tried to imagine waking up in my home, in my

life, but it was all gone. I could remember the world, the real world of soft, round shapes, of people and houses and cars and lives. I just couldn't remember me in it.

My vision narrowed as an invisible fist closed around my lungs. "Who am I?"

Tension pulsed up through the veins in my neck. I could feel the skin on my face, the roots of my teeth. Dizzy, nauseous, I staggered back against the base of the hill. What was my name? What did I look like? Was I old? Was I young?

Looking down at my boxy body, I couldn't determine anything. Was I a man or a woman? Was I even human?

"What am I?"

The thread snapped. My mind collapsed.

Where? Who? What? And now the final question.

"Why!?" I screeched up at the bright square sun. "Why can't I remember? Why am I different? Why am I here? Why is all of this happening to me? WHYYY!?"

All I got back was silence. No birds, no waves, not even the rustle of wind through those angular excuses for trees. Nothing but pure, punishing silence.

And then . . .

GRRRP.

The sound was so small I wasn't sure I'd heard it.

GRRRP.

I definitely heard it that time, and felt it, too. It was coming from inside me. My tummy was rumbling.

I'm hungry.

That was all I needed to break my downward spiral. Something to do, something simple and clear to focus on, and next to breathing, there's nothing clearer or simpler than eating.

GRRRP, growled my stomach, as if to say, "I'm waiting."

I shook my head violently, trying to get the blood back in my cheeks, and looked down at my body to see if I had anything to eat. I'd been so shocked the first time I'd seen myself that I might have missed something earlier. Maybe I had a waterproof phone in my pocket, or even a wallet with my ID.

I didn't have either, or even pockets. But what I did find was a thin belt, painted the same color as my pants—another reason I'd missed it the first time—with four flat pouches on either side. Each pouch was empty, but while going through them, I suddenly realized I could feel the slight pressure of something resting gently on my back.

I call it a "backpack" but it didn't have any straps or hooks or anything that should have held it in place. It was just stuck there, and like the belt and my painted-on clothes, I couldn't take it off. All I could do was reach back and swing it to the front.

"Crazy dream," I said, coming back to the only mental crutch I had. The pack's inside was lined with twenty-seven small pouches, just like those on the belt, and also totally empty.

So much for taking inventory, I thought, as the feeling of hunger grew constant. That meant foraging for food. I looked around for something, anything, that looked remotely edible. At first, the only thing I could find appeared to be one-block-high blades of rectangular grass. They grew in ones and twos on the green-covered dirt behind the beach. I reached down to one sprouting right at my feet, but somehow I couldn't pick it up. Instead I just swiped clumsily in a rapid punching motion.

Anxiety welled up in me again. It was one thing to have a strange-looking body, but a whole new crisis to discover that that body wouldn't obey! I tried again, missing the grass, and again, and when I finally connected, my fist smashed my target to oblivion. And I do mean oblivion. The tall green stalks didn't just fall over or break, they disappeared. One quick crunching noise and poof, gone.

"Aw, c'mon!" I pouted, looking at this angular appendage. "Just work, will ya?" For some reason, pleading with my hand wasn't the answer. Neither was trying to repeat the same fruitless motion on another identical clump of grass.

I've heard, although I can't remember where, that the definition of insanity is doing the same thing over and over again hoping for a different result. I don't know if that's true for some people, but for me, it was pretty darn close.

"Just work!" I grunted angrily, punching the grass like it had swung first. "Work. Work. WORK!" It was starting again, the mental slide. My mind was balancing on a thin tightrope at that moment, and I really needed some kind of win.

I didn't get one, exactly, but I did break the cycle by accidentally, literally, breaking the ground. On the fourth try, I hit so hard and for so long that I didn't only destroy the little green blades, but also knocked away a whole block of dirt beneath them.

"Whoa . . ." I stammered, frustration replaced with curiosity.

At first I didn't see the block, just the block-sized hole it'd disappeared into. I peered into the divot and saw a cube floating at the bottom—actually hovering off the ground—and much smaller than it had been. I reached in to pick it up and didn't get halfway there before it flew up at me.

I stumbled back with a surprised "whoa!" and looked down at the cube in my hand. It felt like dirt, coarse and dry with a few little pebbles in it. I tried squeezing my hand and felt it give without crumbling. I brought it up to my face and sniffed. It smelled just like dirt.

I sniffed again, and suddenly felt comforted. Everything was alien up till that point; everything around me, including me. This wasn't. This one sensation was familiar. I could feel my neck muscles relaxing, my jaw unclenching. Hey, I'm not embarrassed to say that I took another four or five good, long, tranquilizing whiffs of that dirt block, and I'm also not embarrassed to say that in between each inhale, I glanced over my shoulder just to see that no one was looking.

I won't say the experience made everything better, but it did give me the confidence to try opening my fingers to drop the block on the ground. And it did. And I felt even better.

"Well, all right," I exhaled, "At least I have the power to drop things." Not a huge win, I know, but something. Some tiny bit of control.

I watched the little dirt cube hover at my feet for a second, then reached out to pick it up again. I didn't flinch the second time it jumped to meet me.

"Okay," I said, taking a cautious breath. "If I can drop you, maybe I can . . ." I moved the cube down to one of the pouches on my belt, and sighed deeply as it obediently dropped inside.

"So," I said, smiling down at the belt, "stuff—well, dirt, at least—shrinks small enough for you to carry it. Weird, but maybe useful in this w . . . dream." I couldn't say "world" yet. I was still way too fragile.

Grrrp, bubbled my stomach, reminding me it was still there.

"Right," I said, and took the cube back out of my belt. "And since I can't eat you, and can't think of a reason to carry you around . . ."

I held the shrunken box out to the hole where I'd dug it up. At maybe a pace or two away, it jumped right out of my hand, swelled back up to its original shape, and snapped into place as if nothing had happened. Well, almost nothing; digging it out had taken off its green cover.

"Hmmm," I hummed and tried digging it up again. Sure enough, a few punches drove it right into my hand. When I put it down this time, I tried setting it next to the hole instead of inside it. Again it sprang back to its normal size, sitting securely on the ground.

I hummed again, my newfound calm allowing the wheels to turn. Something about setting the block down in a new place reminded me of a buried memory. I don't think it was a memory specific to me, but rather to the not-dream world. Something about little kids playing with blocks, making things, building.

"If everything here is made of blocks," I said to the newly re-planted cube, "and all these blocks keep their shape, could I stack them into things I want to build?"

GRRRP, came a particularly angry protest from down south.

"Right," I told my stomach, and turning to the block, said, "Maybe later. I gotta eat."

I figured I'd give the grass one more try before moving on. I'm glad I did. On this fifth attempt, the vanishing clump left a collection of hovering seeds. *Finally*, I thought and tried picking them up. One weird minor quirk of this dream was that I could only grab all six seeds at the same time, and wasn't able to hold them individually. Another weird, and ridiculously major, quirk was that I wasn't able to consume them. My hand just froze there, inches from my mouth, and wouldn't let me eat.

"Really?" I said, and tried to move my face to my hand instead. That didn't work either, like an invisible force field was holding them apart.

"Really," I repeated sarcastically, feeling all the frustration and anger rising up. "Fine!" My arm cocked to throw the seeds away.

What stopped me was the block of dirt I'd just been experimenting with. When I'd set it down a few minutes ago, the green cover top was missing. Now it was back. The turfy layer had re-grown.

That fast? I thought, looking down at the seeds. *Do all plants grow that fast? Maybe I could try planting these seeds.*

And boy did I try! I tried every way I could think of. I dropped the seeds back onto the ground, but they just hovered. I punched them into the soil, but that just unearthed another block. And after setting that block down, in a new position aboveground, I even tried pushing the seeds into the side. Nothing worked.

"Why won't . . ." I hissed through clenched teeth, then stopped myself. Going down the "why" path would lead me right back to a full-blown meltdown.

"Keep going," I said with a huff. "Don't give up."

Dropping the seeds into a belt pouch, I desperately looked around for another option. Any other food source, any distraction . . .

The trees!

I ran over to the closest one, trying to peel away sections of the bark. Do people eat bark? Maybe, but I couldn't. My hands wouldn't let me grab the light-and-dark-striped brown cover. They also wouldn't let me climb the waist-thick trunk up to the square bunches of small, mini-cubed leaves.

I didn't give up; I couldn't afford to. "If this is a dream," I said, "then I can just fly up and get some!"

Fist raised, eyes up, I leapt into the air . . . and came down just as quick. But in that crucial moment, suspended in midair, something truly magical happened. I tried punching at the leaves above me, and even though they were a block or two away, I felt my fist impact.

I began hesitantly striking up above me. "I can reach?"

Sure enough, though my actual arm didn't stretch, from four full block lengths away I could still hit the dappled cubes above my head. "I can reach!" I shouted and began bashing at the leaves. Creeping insanity faded with each empowering punch. "Yeah!" I belted as the first cube vanished, dropping a red, shiny, semi-rounded fruit into my hand. "THAT'S what I'm talkin' about!"

And this time, my body let me eat. *Maybe that's the key,* I thought, crunching on the fruit's crispy sweetness and feeling the juice run down my throat. *Maybe my hand will only let me eat what's edible.*

It might not have looked exactly like an apple, but it tasted just like one. And if I thought the scent of the earth was comforting, this new sensation was so overpowering, I actually felt a sting at the corners of my eyes.

"Keep going," I said as the entire apple disappeared into my welcoming stomach. "Never give up!"

Without realizing it, I'd just learned something. Call it a mantra or a life lesson or whatever, but they were words to live by, and they'd be the first of many on this strange and wonderful journey: Never give up.

CHAPTER 2

PANIC DROWNS THOUGHT

Using my new "power," I knocked out the other leaf blocks on the rest of the trees. I not only came away with two more apples, but a critical discovery about my belt and pack.

It happened right after the first apple, when I was boxing the leaves. Instead of dropping fruit, I got a small sapling. "On strike again?" I asked my frozen hand, and dropped the mini-tree into my belt. Seconds later, when I got a second one, I absentmind-edly stuffed it into the same pouch. That's when I realized that they'd not only shrunk, but flattened and stacked themselves together like playing cards. "Well now," I said with a smile, "this might actually be helpful."

That turned out to be an understatement. By the time I'd finished stripping all three trees, I managed to stack twelve compressed saplings in just one compartment. And, I might add, at zero weight!

Looking over the additional pouches in my pack, I thought, *I can carry a whole warehouse worth of stuff! Which means . . .*

"Which means," I said, scowling at the belt, my mood deflating like stacked saplings, "Until I find stuff worth carrying, you're as helpful as a wind-powered fan."

There's gotta be more apple trees, I thought, staring up at the cliff. Through panicked eyes, it'd initially looked like an impassable barrier. Now, calmer, confident, and well-fed, I could see that it was more like a steep slope than a sheer wall.

Who knows what else is over there, I thought, hiking up square dirt cubes. If I'd only thought clearly instead of being such a total dweeb, I wouldn't have trapped myself on this side of the island in the first place.

In fact, maybe it wasn't an island after all. Maybe this beach was the start of a whole continent! Don't get me wrong, I hadn't abandoned the notion of all this being just a dream. But still, part of me couldn't help wishing to come up over the top of the hill to see a ranger station, or a town, or a giant city, or . . .

There wasn't.

I stood on the even, green summit and stared with crushing disappointment at the rest of an uninhabited island.

The land stretched out like a claw, two wooded pincers nearly enclosing a round, shallow lagoon. I couldn't judge how large the island was. By that point, I still wasn't very good at measuring by blocks. But it couldn't have been too big because I could definitely see the end of it under the late afternoon sun. And with the sinking orange square, so went my spirits as well.

Just like in the water, I thought I was alone.

And just like in the water, I was wrong.

"Moo." The sound made me jump.

"Wha . . . ?" I said, nervously looking all around. "Who . . . Who's there?"

"Moo," came the sound again, pulling my eyes to the base of the hill. It was an animal, black and white, with a body as rectangular as its surroundings.

I picked my way down the western slope, which was easier and more gradual than the treacherous eastern side, and walked right up to the fearless creature. Studying it more closely, I could see that it wasn't entirely black and white. *Gray horns, pink inside the ears, and a pink shallow sack below the stomach . . .*

"You gotta be a cow," I said, and the "moo" I got was the best sound I'd heard all day. "You don't know how happy I am to see you," I sighed. "I mean, hey, I know it's still just a dream and all, but it just feels so good not to be—" the word stuck in my throat, stinging my nose and eyes—"alone."

"Baa," answered the cow.

"Wait, what?" I asked, stepping closer. "Are you, like, bilingual or . . ."

"Baa," said the animal, but not the one in front of me. I looked up and past the cow, toward the sound's true owner. It was rectangular—*duh*—but a little shorter and practically all black.

I'd almost missed it in the dim light of the early evening. Now, as I approached the darkening woods, another animal, as white as the clouds above, stepped out from behind its black twin. Despite their straight, flat outlines, I could see the barest details of woolly coats.

"You're sheep," I said, smiling, and reached out to pet one. I wasn't thinking. I didn't mean to punch.

The animal yelped, flashed pinkish red, and took off running through the wood. "Oh, sorry!" I called after it. "Sorry little sheep!" I felt so bad that I turned to its unfazed friend and babbled, "I didn't mean it, really. I still don't know how to use this body, ya know?"

"Cluckcluckcluck," came an answer to my left. Two small birds, each about a block high, were pecking the nearby ground. They had short, skinny legs, plump bodies covered with white feathers, and small heads ending in flat orange beaks.

"I'm not sure if you're chickens," I told them. "You do have kinda duckish features." They glanced up at me for a second and clucked. "But you sound like chickens," I continued, "so I guess calling you chickens makes more sense than . . . chicke-ducks."

The word gave me a little chuckle, which quickly became a real guffaw. It felt good to laugh, to let out all the crazy tension of the day.

That's when I heard a new sound.

"Guuugh."

It was a throaty, phlegmy gargle that sent chills up my spine. I looked all around, trying to figure out the source. Sound on this island seemed to be coming from every direction. I stood there listening, wishing the chickens would shut up.

Then I smelled it. Mold and rot. Like a dead rat in an old sock. I didn't see the figure until it was only a dozen or so paces away. At first I thought it was another person, dressed just like me, and I took an automatic step forward.

Then, just as instinctively, I stopped and backed away. Its clothes were ragged and filthy. Its flesh was a mottled green. Its eyes, if you could call them eyes, were nothing but lifeless black points in a flat, unmoving face. Memories flooded my mind, images of creatures I'd known from stories but had never seen in person. And now here it was, approaching with outstretched arms.

This was a zombie!

I tried to retreat, bumping against a tree. The zombie closed. I dodged. Rotted fists smashed into my chest, throwing me back. Pain shot through my body. I gasped. It lunged. I fled.

Numb with fear, I sprinted for the hill. I wasn't thinking, wasn't planning. Terror drove my every step. Something "clacked" in the darkness behind me, followed by a noise like whipped air. Something smacked into the tree in front of me. A feather-tipped, quivering stick. An *arrow*! Was the zombie armed? I hadn't noticed. I just kept running.

Something red flashed to my right: a cluster of eyes followed by a clipped hiss. I scampered up the slope of the hill, glancing back only when I was at the summit. In the pale light of a rising square moon, I could see that the zombie was still coming. It was already at the bottom of the slope and beginning to climb up after me.

Throat closing in fright, I tore my way down the eastern cliff. I slipped, fell to the bottom, and heard a sickening crack.

"Rrrr," I hissed as bolts of agony stabbed through my ankle.

Where to go? What to do? Should I jump back into the ocean and try to swim away? I froze at the edge of the blackened water. What if that squid was still out there, and what if it'd gotten hungry?

Another moan echoed across the starry night. I turned to see the zombie's head poke over the top of the hill.

Frantically I looked for somewhere to go. Someplace to hide.

My eyes flicked back and forth, settling on the single block of earth I'd dug out earlier in the day. From it came the spark of a desperate idea. Digging!

As the zombie started down the slope, I ran to the cliff below it and furiously tore into the earth. One-two-three-four punches and the first block in front of me came away. One-two-three-four and the one behind it popped free.

I could hear the ghoul approaching, each groan growing louder. One-two-three-four, one-two-three-four. I cleared four earthen blocks right in front of me, two above and below. Just enough for me to squeeze into the space.

Deeper, my mind screamed. *Get deeper!*

And if fate could talk, it would have sneered and said, "You're not going anywhere."

My fists bounced off something cold and hard. I'd hit solid rock. A few pointless punches told me I was trapped, the monster barely seconds away.

I spun, saw the zombie, and set down a block of dirt between us. The ghoul reached over, smashing me in the chest. I flew back, hitting the stone cliff. Chest aching, gasping for breath, I jammed the second soil cube on top of the first.

Darkness fell. I was buried alive.

My tomb shut out light but not sound. Zombie moans still rang in my ears. What if it could dig? What if I'd only delayed death by seconds?

"Go away!" I shouted helplessly. "Please just leave me alone!"

Gagging growls answered.

"Please!" I pleaded.

Unfeeling, uncaring, unstoppable moans answered.

"Wake up," I whispered. "I've gotta wake up, wake up, WAKE UP!"

In desperation I started jumping up and down, hitting my head against the ceiling, trying to jolt myself awake.

"WAKEUPWAKEUPWAKEUP!"

I fell back against the stone wall, head throbbing, eyes burning, chest heaving in rapid, panicked sobs.

"Why?" I whimpered. "Why can't I wake up?"

And just then the zombie barked a deep, violent groan. *"Because it's not a dream."*

No, the creature wasn't talking to me. I'd put words in its decayed mouth, words that I knew I needed to hear.

"This isn't a dream," I imagined hearing from the mobile corpse, *"and it's not an injury or a hallucination. This is a real place, a real world, and you're going to have to accept that to survive."*

"You're right," I said to the ghoul, knowing I was talking to myself but still thinking that talking to a dead guy was somehow saner. "This isn't happening in my head. This is happening."

The fragment of a half-remembered song floated through the fog of my amnesia. Something about finding yourself in a strange place. I couldn't remember all the lyrics, but one stuck clearly in my mind:

You may ask yourself, Well, how did I get here?

"I don't know," I admitted. "I don't know how I got here or even where 'here' is. Another planet? Another dimension? I don't know, but I know there's no point in denying it anymore."

And with that acceptance came this huge wave of calm, and with the calm came a new mantra.

"Panic drowns thought," I told the zombie, "so it's time to stop panicking and start figuring out how to survive."

CHAPTER 3

DON'T ASSUME ANYTHING

"What's my next move?" I asked the darkness. Given that I was trapped, literally with my back to the wall, with a snarling corpse just a handful of dirt away, the options seemed pretty limited.

For a long while, I tried to just focus on my breathing, clearing my mind, letting the ideas flow. Ironically the first clear thought I had was that my breathing might be using up all my air.

How much did I have? Was I already suffocating? What did suffocation feel like? I tried to sense any changes in my body, any feelings that weren't there before. And that's when I noticed that all the pain from my injuries was gone. Both my head and ankle felt fine. My stomach, on the other hand, felt completely empty. I chomped down another apple, trying to make sense of what was happening.

Am I losing oxygen to the brain, I wondered, *or did I just heal super fast? Seriously, am I a superhero?* The thought gave me a sudden rush of hope.

The zombie groaned.

"Is that it?" I asked the ghoul. "Does this world give me hyper-healing, and do the apples, or any food, have something to do with it?"

Another noncommittal groan.

"You don't have to answer," I said. "I'll figure everything out, because that's what it takes to survive here, right? This is a whole new world with a whole new set of rules, like punching from a distance or a little bag that holds a lot of stuff."

Deeper breathing brought greater calm, and greater calm brought clearer thinking. "I just need to figure out what's what," I stated matter-of-factly, "and I'll do that as soon as I bust outta here!"

On cue, the zombie groaned back.

"And when I do, you'll be waiting, so I'll need some kind of weapon to defend myself. A club, or a spear, or—"

The zombie gave a quick, high-pitched growl I hadn't heard before.

"Hey," I said, putting my ear to the dirt, "what gives?"

Had it heard me? Were we having an actual conversation?

The sharp, harsh growls kept coming, like the creature was reacting to something, like it was in pain.

"You okay?" I asked reflexively. "Hey, I'm sorry if talking about weapons hurts your feelings or something, but, in all fairness, you are tryin' to kill me so . . ." Halfway through my babbling, I noticed that the sounds were gone.

"Hello?" I called out to silence.

I thought I could smell something seeping through the dirt. Smoke?

Was the zombie building a fire outside my hole and trying to smoke me out? Could zombies *do* that?

I had to know. If sitting here meant dying of smoke inhalation, I had to take my chances out in the open. Heart pounding, I knocked out the dirt cube in front of my face, and blinked hard in the light of the square morning sun.

I couldn't see the zombie, but I could still smell its rotten stench, now mixed with the strong scent of smoke. I tore out the second block and stepped cautiously onto the beach. I looked right, then left, then down, and wrinkled my nose. A chunk of putrid meat was hovering at my feet. I picked it up nervously, and winced at the utter grossness.

The fringes were charred like a burnt burger, and I didn't need to ask where the smoky smell had come from.

I darted across the sand, thinking that this was a trap and the zombie might be waiting on the hill just above me. It wasn't. The coast, literally, was clear. "Hey, Dead Dude!" I shouted, holding up the hunk of rot. "You forgot yourself?"

I waited a tense minute, hoping the chunk's owner wouldn't come slouching back over the hill. It didn't. This bit of burnt grody guts had to be all that was left.

But why?

The sun. But didn't daylight kill only vampires? Maybe in my world. "But," I said to the chunk, "we're not in my world, and I can't assume anything." And just as I said that, my eyes fell on my small, cliffside hidey-hole. Specifically, I noticed the two-block-long, one-block-wide ceiling of dirt. Why hadn't it collapsed on top of me? What was holding it up?

I went back into the hole and punched out the two earthen blocks above my head. Then, moving away so they wouldn't land on me, I put them right back in place. And they stuck!

"Cool!" I smiled, feeling a surge of confidence. Other than hyper-healing, the ability to stick dirt blocks to each other was a huge advantage of this world. It meant that I could build a shelter without nails or cement or whatever kept houses up.

That's assuming, of course, that there wouldn't be a natural sanctuary waiting for me somewhere out there. I hiked to the top of the hill, scanned the entire length of the island—checking the north and south slopes just to be sure—then heaved a heavy sigh of disappointment. There was no cave, no hole, no move-right-in fortress.

I noticed the cow, two of them actually, grazing at the bottom of the western slope, munching and mooing to their hearts' content.

"Well," I called down to them, my eyes now fixed on the trees, "at least I was right about the sun chasing those monsters away."

The light had definitely banished whatever had been lurking in the woods the night before. But where had they gone? And for that matter, where had they come from? Did they walk out of the sea at dusk, or crawl out of the ground like in some cheesy horror film?

I'd probably know a lot sooner than I wanted to. Even though dawn had only been a few minutes ago, the sun was already halfway to noon.

"How short are the days here?" I asked the contented cows. And if they could have spoken, they probably would have answered, "Short enough to stop wasting time."

"Thanks," I said sarcastically, then turned to climb back down what I was now calling Disappointment Hill. For a moment I hesitated, wondering if I should build a signal fire. Isn't that what people did when they were marooned on an island? Maybe, but I had no idea how to do it.

What I did know how to do, though, was dig. Using nothing but my hands I punched out enough dirt blocks to spell the word "HELP!" *Maybe a low-flying airplane or even a high-flying satellite will see it,* I thought. *Someone'll come along.* I was still clinging to the idea that somebody was going to swoop in and save me, that all I had to do was last a night or two until they did. I might have accepted that this was a whole new world, but I didn't stop to consider what that really meant. I would though, later, when I got myself lost at sea . . . again.

But I'm getting ahead of myself.

With a watchful eye on the sun, I trudged back down the eastern slope. I thought about building a dirt hut out from my hole in the cliff. But when I looked at the narrow opening, I figured it'd be a lot safer just to burrow deeper. That way I'd have a whole hill between me and danger, instead of a few flimsy dirt walls. But how to do that?

I couldn't tunnel through stone with my bare hands. Could I? *Don't assume anything,* I reminded myself, raising my fist to the smooth gray wall. *You already have a "distance punch" super-power. Maybe that punch can break rocks.*

Turns out it can't.

"OW, OW, OW," I yelped with each hit. Yes, it's true that this world lets flesh do damage to solid rock, and yes, after battering for a while it did look like I was making progress. The gray cube didn't crack, though, not like it would in my world. What I saw were little, multicolored mini blocks spreading out from my impact point. But the moment I rested my bruised, aching hands, all the damage to the rock sealed right back up.

"Aw, man!" I shouted and angrily decked the rock again, which forced out another painful "OWWW!"

Apparently I wasn't the only thing in this world with hyper-healing.

"What do I need to take you out?" I asked the silent, mocking stone.

Some kind of tool was the obvious answer, like the castaways in all those stories. But they usually had a whole shipwreck of supplies, or a hatchet, or at least a talking volleyball.

What did I have? Fuzzy memories and a backpack full of nothing.

Well, almost nothing.

I tried hitting the stone wall with things I'd collected: saplings, dirt cubes, even zombie flesh. For all I knew, this world gave any one of them the power of a jackhammer. None of them worked, but the sapling gave me the idea to try ripping a piece of harder, stronger wood from the leafless trees behind me.

I went over to the closest trunk and punched out the bottom section.

"Timmmberrr!" I shouted, then let out a confused huff.

Not only was the tree still upright, it was standing with nothing connecting it to the ground.

"Look," I said, negotiating with the suspended column, "blocks and zombies are one thing, but gravity!?"

The floating trunk didn't move.

"Okay"—I nodded, throwing up my dice-shaped hands—"your world, your rules."

A few seconds later, I saw how true those words were.

I tried bashing the cubed log against the cliff and got nothing more than a sore hand.

I winced and, without thinking, started to pass the log to my left hand in order to give my right one a break.

"Wha . . . ?" My square eyes widened as my left hand opened to reveal a luminous grid. There were two lines, up-down, side-to-side, dividing my palm into four sections. As the shrunken log fell into the bottom left section, the glowing image of four stacked wooden planks floated up from my open right hand.

"All right," I said nervously, not sure if what was happening was good or bad. I tried slowly closing my fingers. The planks grew solid just as the log in my left hand vanished.

"All right!" I said with growing zeal.

In addition to the ability to heal quickly, punch things from a distance, and stick blocks to themselves without supports, somehow this world allowed me to transform raw materials into finished products in seconds. How long would that task have taken in my world? How many hours of chopping, measuring, sawing, and sanding? And that's assuming I already knew how to do any of that. This world let me be a master crafter just by changing hands!

What can I make with these, I wondered, passing the stacked planks to my left hand. This time a tiny wooden mini-cube floated above my right.

"A button," I breathed. Not the kind for clothes, but the kind you press. Head spinning, literally dizzy with new discoveries, I could only imagine what would happen when I pressed it. Would the button transform whatever it was stuck to into something completely different? Would it transform me? Or maybe it would raise up a giant, gleaming fortress that held a white-haired spirit who would answer all my questions and teach me how to use my powers. Hadn't that happened in a movie?

I closed my hand on the button, grabbing it from the air and sticking it to the suspended tree.

. . . was this the key to sending me home!?

"I'm ready," I shouted to the heavens, my shaking hand reaching out for the all-powerful, all-important button.

CLICK.

"Right." I sighed, hearing the *wah-wah* of a trombone in my head. "So much for all the answers."

But looking down at the remaining wood, I said, "But maybe you've still got a few."

I spread the three planks out among the four spaces in my hand, and got nothing. But as soon as I took one away, the other two—sitting one above the other—projected the image of four long sturdy sticks.

"A club!" I shouted, grabbing them from the air. Putting three in my belt, I swung the fourth like a demented Neanderthal. "Me strong! Me have weapon!"

Then, still in character, I looked back at the stone wall and growled, "Me also have rock breaker!"

I should have quit experimenting right then and there. I

should have gone back to digging out my underground shelter. But, big surprise, I didn't.

"Just a few more experiments," I said, turning my back to the rock wall, "and then I'll get to work."

Since the one remaining plank was only good for making buttons, I slipped it into my belt and started bashing down the rest of the suspended tree.

I divided the new planks among all the four sections of my hand, and gaped in wonder at the ghostly image they produced. This cube seemed to have all kinds of tools hanging from its sides. "Here we go!" I shouted, grabbing this new game changer. It didn't matter that the tools were as painted-on as my clothes. The whole workbench, or "crafting table," was a tool. Its top was laid out in nine sections that looked and acted exactly like my left hand.

"Aw, yeah!" I sang, doing what would now become my signature victory dance. I hopped a few times, spun once, hopped again, then reached for my remaining wood planks and threw them on the table.

"Let's get crafting!"

My first few results were, let's just say, less than stellar. Placing two planks side by side got me a thin, almost full block-wide square. Placing the square on the ground and stepping on it got me the same anticlimactic CLICK as the button. Three planks across got me six half-cube-thick slabs. Doubling them to six planks got me two similar slabs but with square holes cut in the corners. I placed one down on the ground, walked around it, stepped on it to no effect, then tried to punch it back up again.

Instead of shrinking into my hand, the slab tilted upward like a hatch. *Awesome*, I thought, *now I don't need hinges.*

And this theory was further proved when I tried a combination of six upright planks, and got three full-size doors.

I set one down on the ground, saw that it remained standing, then reached out to open it. And yes, the freestanding door swung open with a totally normal creaking sound.

Now, I know what you're thinking, okay? Why not just quit the crafting and get right to work making a house for this door, or, at the very least, dig a rabbit hole in the ground and cover it with the hatch? Believe me, I thought about it, and I really was going to get to it eventually. But I couldn't stop without making the hand tools I saw on the sides of the crafting table. I mean, if this world had put them there, then they had to exist. So why wasn't I able to make them?

I felt like those hand tools were just one more combination away. After all, I'd made so much progress, and even picked up another lesson in the process: Figuring out the rules turns them from enemies into friends.

"Just a few more tries," I promised, placing a plank on every section of the table. When that got me nothing, I happened, by sheer chance, to take the middle one out first.

Instantly the image of a box appeared, and I don't mean a box-shaped something, I mean an actual box. I put it down in front of me, and opened the hingeless lid. It seemed to be a fixed version of my pack with just as many compartments.

"Figures," I huffed. "Tons more storage and nothing to store."

And on the subject of emptiness, my next experiment—three planks in a V—got me four empty wooden bowls. Instinctively, I pictured filling them with all kinds of soups and stews. Mouth watering, I reached for an apple.

For the first time, though, my hand refused to move, and a second later I realized why. I wasn't hungry. This world only let me eat when I needed to, not when I wanted to. "Well, that's not fun," I told the apple. "But at least I'll never waste food . . . if I find any more."

Looking at the leafless tree trunks, I wondered if I shouldn't try searching for more apples before it got dark. But before I did that, I really had to get moving on that shelter. But before I did *that . . .*

Just one more try.

I put another load of planks on the crafting table, adding a few more to change the V to a U.

At first I thought I'd just made another bowl, but larger and more oval shaped, like a tub or . . .

"A BOAT!" I shouted, yanking it from the ether. With it still miniaturized in my hand, I ran up and over Disappointment Hill.

"Hey, guys!" I shouted to the grazing animals. "Check this out! I got a boat!"

The sheep and cows glanced up casually, then got back to more important munching.

"And a heartfelt farewell to you, too!" I said, running past them to the northern beach.

I set the tiny model tub in the water and it instantly grew into a full-sized skiff. Climbing aboard, I couldn't believe how stable it was. No rocking, no bobbing, totally smooth. Since there was no motor or sail, I figured the only way to get going was by paddling. I leaned forward to dip my hands in the water, and the boat suddenly began to move. *All I gotta do is lean*, I thought, smiling as the little craft picked up speed.

Escape! Freedom!

"Yeah!" I yelled, turning back to give my island prison a final goodbye. I intended to shout something snarky like "So long, suckers!" but stopped when I saw the last bit of land shrink to a speck on the horizon. I sat up slightly, slowing the boat. I squinted for land up ahead. There wasn't any. I glanced back at the island. It was gone. I came to a full stop, looked in every direction, and saw nothing but sky and sea.

And that's when reality set in.

What was I thinking? Where was I going? Escaping the island didn't mean escaping the world. At least back there I kinda knew what I was dealing with. Out here it was all unknown. This is what I should have considered when carving my "HELP!" sign on the hill. Back when I was dry and safe.

What if there wasn't any other land? Or what if the land

didn't have any people? Or what if the people were as dangerous as zombies? Or what if there were only zombies, and those other monsters I'd seen last night? Or worse?

Gulping down stomach acid, I spun around and sped back to the island. Only the island wasn't there. Was I going in the right direction? I zigged this way and that, hoping for just the faintest hint of green.

Nothing.

I was lost.

"Stupid," I hissed, furious with myself for making such a thoughtless mistake.

I'd been so eager to get home that I'd blown my one chance to survive. Now I was right back where I started, helpless and hopeless. No way was I getting out of this one.

Sooner or later I'd eat my last apple then starve slowly under the baking sun. Or maybe I'd be eaten by a squid. Maybe one was coming for me now!

I could almost feel the hungry arms rising from the depths, ready to smash my boat and drag me under. Hopefully I'd drown before they tore me apart.

Drown . . .

"Panic drowns thought," I whispered, feeling the strength in my words. The enemy wasn't rising squids, but my own rising hysteria, squeezing my chest, clouding my brain.

"Panic drowns thought!" I shouted. "And I'm *not* going to drown!"

I reached into my belt, not for the apple, but for a cube of dirt. Fittingly, I still had plenty from the "HELP!" sign. I closed my eyes and inhaled its rich, grounding scent.

"Let's go find the rest of you," I told it. "We have to be close. There's no current, and the breeze can't've blown us too far off course."

The breeze.

So far I'd only noticed it gusting east to west. I looked up to the clouds and matched their movement with the line of the setting sun.

"Now we know east and west," I said with growing confidence, "and since we started from the island's north beach, keeping the sun to the right means heading south."

I put the dirt back in my belt and leaned cautiously forward . . .

. . . and there it was, the top of Disappointment Hill. I sighed in relief, leaning as far forward as I could.

The boat shot headlong onto the beach, smashing into planks and sticks against the sandy northern shore.

I didn't care.

"Made it," I whispered, wishing my body could let me kiss the ground.

"Moo," called an approaching cow, its voice heavy with criticism.

"I know," I said, getting out of the water and collecting the remains of my boat. "I wasn't thinking."

"Moo," said the cow.

"You're right," I answered. "I've gotta think *before* I act, and that doesn't just mean figuring out my next move. I need a clear, long-term strategy if I'm gonna survive this world."

"Moo," agreed the cow.

"I've gotta focus on covering the basics," I continued. "Stockpiling food, building a secure shelter, crafting tools and weapons and whatever else I'll need to make my life more comfortable."

I began pacing back and forth, emphatically gesturing to the watching animal. "I've gotta turn this island into a comfort zone, a safe space where I can learn all I can about how this world works. And then, when I've got all the basics covered, I can start asking the really big questions, like how I got here, and how I get home."

And just as I considered those big questions, an even bigger, scarier one came to mind. "Can I do it?" I asked. "All by myself, with no one to help me?"

I stared down at my painted shoes. "No one to protect or guide or"—I could barely get the words out—"take care of me?"

I closed my eyes, trying to remember something, anything, about who I was. "If I'm a kid," I said, trembling, "then grown-ups must have done a lot for me. And if I'm a grown-up, then I still don't remember doing much for myself." Memories of that other world flashed before my anguished eyes, memories of machines and luxuries and clicking a screen to order anything I wanted. "I think my world did a lot for me, so many people doing so many different jobs that nobody had to worry about doing everything."

I looked up into the cow's face. "Can I do everything? Can I take care of me?"

The square animal gave a long, low "moo," which I took for "What other choice is there?"

"Only one," I answered. "To curl up and die."

I sighed hard. "Which I won't do."

"I choose to take care of myself," I proclaimed, as desperation morphed into determination. "I choose to believe in myself!"

"Moo," said the cow, sounding to me like, "Now you're talkin'!"

"I can do this!" I bellowed boldly. "I can and I WILL! I . . . I . . ." I noticed the sun had almost set. "I gotta get outta here!"

Confidence vanished as I raced out of the woods. How long did I have before the night terrors rose again? How long before they hunted me down?

CHAPTER 4

DETAILS MAKE THE DIFFERENCE

By the time I reached the top of the hill, my mind was like quivering Jell-O.

Turning to the setting sun, I begged, "Not yet. Please don't leave me alone with the monsters. Stay a little longer. Please don't abandon me!"

"Moo!" cried the distant cow, as if to say, "Stop whimpering and move your butt!"

And I did. I rushed down the eastern slope to the beach, over to my shallow hole. I started banging at the stone cliff with my digging stick, and suddenly felt my heart sink. It was taking for-ever. If I'd only tested the stick earlier, if I hadn't just assumed it'd work . . .

"Uuuhhh." The soft moan floated through the night air. An-other zombie was coming.

I jumped at the sound, dropped my stick, and looked franti-cally around. Just like the lesson about not assuming, I'd also completely lost the mantra about drowned thought. I was in full panic mode now, a trapped rat waiting for an undead cat.

"Guuuhhh," came a louder, closer moan.

I looked down for my stick. It was gone, maybe hovering close by, but in the growing darkness, I couldn't see it.

"Gahhh," gargled the ghoul.

I looked up at the hilltop and saw my foe.

I reached into my belt for one of the other three sticks. My hand brushed the earthen cubes.

Build! The zombie was starting down the slope toward me. Something glinted in its grasp. A weapon?

I raced to create a hovel around myself, slamming dirt blocks down into walls. Yes, I suppose I could have, and should have, just blocked myself back up in the hole. It would have been the quicker, easier choice. But the thought of being buried alive again, passively pinned in an upright grave, was enough to squeeze the air from my chest

The zombie was only twenty steps away. I jammed the door into place.

Ten steps. I finished the walls and realized I didn't have enough dirt for the roof.

Five steps.

I grabbed a wooden slab from my belt, throwing it up against the corner wall. It thudded with the impact of a rotted foot.

I slapped up slabs and wooden planks, just one step ahead of the slouching ghoul. I fitted the last corner plank, blotting out the stars, thinking I was safe. Then I heard the "oof" as the zombie hit the ground.

Reeking fists began pounding at my door. Heart thumping, I retreated against the far wall. Cold, hard stone pressed against my back. The door in front of me buckled. I could see dark, mini-cubed cracks spreading across its surface. Another few blows would send it crashing down.

"Fine!" I barked. "You wanna fight? C'mon, let's do this!"

Stick in hand, I waited for the door to splinter. And I waited, and waited, and waited . . . and then saw that wood, just like stone, and just like me, could heal. I watched the zombie get within maybe a punch or two of breaking down the thin, buckling barrier, before having to restart the whole process again.

"Yeah," I taunted, "that's right. Now you know how I felt."

Nodding like a proud rooster, I strutted over to the door. "You ain't gettin' in," I sang, "you ain't gettin'—"

Too close.

A moldy arm shot through one of the open squares and socked me right in the throat. "Point taken," I coughed, staggering back. At least it hadn't hit me with whatever was in its other hand.

From a safe distance, I tried to get a better look at the weapon. It wasn't easy, especially in the darkness of my hut. I thought I could see a long, thin wooden handle, similar to my own sticks. Dim moonlight glinted off something at the end. It was flat, roundish, and tapered to a point.

"That's a shovel!" I exclaimed. "How'd you get a shovel?" Then quickly added, "How come I didn't get one?"

I'm not ashamed to say I was jealous. After all that crafting I'd done, I'd made everything but the kind of tools that'd got me crafting in the first place. And now the very thing I'd wanted was right outside my door.

"That's not fair," I pouted.

The zombie growled back, saying what I'm sure anyone would have said to me at that moment, *"Life's not fair, and whining won't make it fair."*

"Yeah, well . . ." I said, cooling down and squinting hard at the shovel. "But how'd you get one anyway?"

The tool's head didn't look wooden. It was lighter, more reflective.

"Is that metal?" I asked.

The ghoul groaned.

"Even if it is, it doesn't help me in here, does it? But . . ."

I squinted at the shovel again, studying it from a whole new angle.

"But if this world lets you combine a wooden handle with something else to make the head," I asked the zombie, "then why can't that head also be made out of wood?"

The zombie groaned again, and I'm 99 percent sure that groan sounded like "Duh!"

Whipping up another crafting table—my original was still outside—I placed a stick on the center square and a wood plank above it.

And got squat.

This time, the zombie moans sounded like laughter.

"What do you expect," I shot back. "Instant success?" Even if I had, I wasn't going to let my undead tormentor know that. "You almost never get something right the first time."

I tried reversing the arrangement, stick above plank, and came up with another big helping of bubkes.

"I'll get it," I reassured the ghoul. "I'm not givin' up." I glanced again at the shovel, making sure I wasn't missing some minor but important detail. I was. A closer look showed me that the shovel's handle was twice as long as my sticks.

I moved the plank to the top center square and placed two sticks below it. "WHOO-HOO!" I howled at a near duplicate of the zombie's shovel.

I snatched it from the air, whooped again, jumped into my victory dance, and promptly banged my head on the low ceiling.

"Laugh it up," I told the zombie, "nothing's gonna spoil this moment."

I pointed the shovel's head at the dirt floor and scooped up a cube with a few quick swipes. "Don't ignore the details," I said. "Details make the difference."

I walked over to the back wall and gave the stone a whack. The wooden blade bounced off harmlessly.

"Just wanted to be sure," I said over my shoulder. "If this thing works for dirt then something else'll work for rocks."

I went to the crafting table and got out all my remaining planks. "You don't have any helpful crafting tips, do you?" I asked the zombie. "How to make, I don't know, a hammer and chisel or a steam drill?"

Dead eyes glared silently back.

"Never mind," I said. "I got this."

I made a couple more sticks and tried arranging them with two more planks into an upside-down L. What I got was a tool similar to a shovel but with a longer, thinner, right angled blade.

"What's this?" I asked the zombie, showing it the strange implement. I thought I remembered seeing something like it back in my world, something to do with soil. I tried to use it like a shovel, digging up a block from the floor. It worked, but not as quickly.

"This world wouldn't give me two digging tools, would it? And why would one work better than the other?"

I tried using the new whatchamacallit against the stone. It worked about as well as my fists. "What's wrong with this thing?" I grumbled, remembering how it felt to punch up grass with my new, frustrating hands. Crazily enough, reconnecting with that feeling got me seriously thinking about how I used my body.

"It's like . . ." I began, searching for the words. "Like I'm in two different minds when I'm doing things. There's . . . I don't know . . . like an aggressive punch mode, and a more passive use mode. Does that make sense?"

"Uhhh," said the zombie.

"I know it sounds ridiculous, like something you'd hear from a mountaintop guru or a little green swamp alien who can lift a spaceship with his mind. But doesn't it kinda make sense?"

Trying to focus my thoughts, I held the strange device against a square in the dirt floor. Restraining the urge to swing it like a shovel, I concentrated on careful thought. The tool swiped quickly but gently across the bare top of the square, taking the first layer of soil with it.

"Balance," I declared. "Survival requires having both aggression and thoughtfulness, hot and cool, yin and . . . whatever the other one's called. Point is to keep them in balance."

"Gruhhh," gurgled the cadaver.

"You should try it sometime," I told it. "The thoughtful part, I mean." And just allowing myself to joke with my would-be killer unlocked another memory of this tool.

"This thing's called a hoe!"

I fished the seeds out of my belt, the ones I'd tried so hard to plant and almost thrown away. I held them out to the soft, moist earth I'd just hoed. The seeds vanished from my hand, filling the soil square with lots of little green shoots.

"Gardening!" I trumpeted. "That's the missing piece! That's why I couldn't plant the seeds yesterday! And if they do grow into something edible, then I've got a renewable source of food!"

"Grehhh," growled the zombie, bashing harmlessly at the door.

"I'm sorry, what was that?" I pretended to ask. "Oh yes, you're right, this night *is* as sucky for you as it is awesome for me. 'Cause while you're stuck out there, doing the same thing over and over again, I just learned tool-making and agriculture, which is, what, like a million years of human evolution in ten minutes?" I sauntered over to the crafting table. "And who knows, maybe by dawn I'll crack the code for cold fusion!"

Three seconds later, I'd made something even better than a nuclear reactor. "A pickaxe!" I announced, holding up the T-shaped triumph. "And all it took was an extra plank!"

Turning from the zombie to the back wall, I tore into the stubborn stone. The pickaxe worked like a dream, plopping out the first block in no time.

"Finally," I sighed, examining the freed rock. It wasn't whole, not like the chunks of dirt. It looked more cobbled together, like all the pieces had reformed.

"And now," I said, glancing back at the zombie's shovel, "let's see if I can improve my tools."

Just as I thought, this world let me combine the block of cobblestone with a couple of sticks into a stone-tipped shovel.

"Figurin' out the rules," I crowed, and tried using it on the dirt floor. The stone tip worked even faster than the wooden version, which could only mean the same for all the others.

Picking out more cobblestone, I went right back to the crafting table.

"Getting an upgrade!" I grinned, gleefully grasping a cobblestone pickaxe.

Just as I thought, the new implement tore through the cliff wall like a shovel through soft earth.

I couldn't really see where I was going; the deepening tunnel was too dark. But the constant flow of cobblestones into my backpack told me I was making serious progress. "Now we're talkin'!" I said, burrowing deeper and deeper into the hill.

"How's it feel, eh?" I asked over my shoulder. "Knowing you and all those other beasties are never gonna get in here!"

My answer came in a familiar sharp, high "gagh."

"Here we go," I said, stepping out of the pitch-black hole and into the growing light of the dirt hut.

Through the square holes in my door, I could see the rising sun and a now-burning zombie. "So you *do* die at dawn!" I said, almost a little sorry for the dying ghoul.

"Gagh-gagh-gagh," it gasped, flashing pink beneath a sheet of flames.

Overcome by curiosity, I edged closer and closer toward the

door. "Oops," I said, as my feet accidentally uprooted the little shoots in the dirt floor. *No matter,* I thought as they jumped right back into my belt, *I'll just replant them outside once the zombie—*

I didn't even get to finish my thought. The burning beast suddenly vanished in a puff of smoke.

CHAPTER 5

BE GRATEFUL FOR WHAT YOU HAVE

I threw open my door just in time to see the last of the smoke dissolve. At my feet was another pile of rotten flesh . . . and no shovel. Whether it had burned with its owner or vanished according to some rule of this world, I couldn't say. I also couldn't waste a minute mourning its loss. This was going to be an awesome day, I could feel it. Last night I'd turned the corner on shelter, and now I was ready to kiss hunger goodbye.

Wooden hoe in hand, I carried the seeds out to a patch of dirt near the shore. Just like before, they jumped right into the freshly tilled soil. How long would it take before they ripened? No way to know. But if they did turn out to be edible, it'd make sense to plant a whole lot more.

Punching the other grass clumps turned up zilch so I decided to spend the morning scrounging. I climbed quickly up the slope of Disappointment Hill and trotted casually down to the central meadow. I wasn't worried about any more zombies this time. I knew the dawn had taken care of them. *A good start to a good day*, I thought, punching up the tall grass. It wasn't long before I'd cleared the whole field, and had three handfuls of seeds to show for it.

"Moo," came a call from the nearby woods, followed by a "baa" and two quick "cluckclucks."

"Hey, g'morning!" I waved to the animals. "You guys would not believe the night I just had."

Bounding happily over, I described my discovery of crafting, and gave a show-and-tell of my tools.

"Cool, eh?" I asked, expecting the usual disinterested glances. "No, I get it," I said, "you can just eat grass as is, but I gotta try replanting these."

I showed them the seeds. The cows and sheep shuffled away. The chickens didn't, though; their heads shot up with rapt attention.

I asked, "What do you want?"

They answered with enthusiastic clucking. "These?" I asked, showing them the seeds. "Are these what you—" I stopped just as a white, oval object popped out from behind one of the birds.

"An egg!" I shouted, switching out the seeds for the hand-sized ball. "Now *this* has to be real food, right?" I asked the chickens. "I mean, why else would this world let you lay an egg if I wasn't allowed to . . ."

I noticed the birds were waddling away. Why had they suddenly lost interest? "Hey, where ya goin'?" I asked. "Something I said?"

I looked away from the birds just in time to see the silent creature gliding between us. It was armless and legless, with a green mottled trunk and short stubby feet.

It all happened so fast. The crackling hiss, the smell of fireworks, the flashing vibrations as the creeping monster swelled like a balloon.

The explosion knocked me backward, lifting me off my feet. Eyes burning, ears ringing, I flew through the air, splashing into the waist-deep water of the lagoon. Waves of pain crashed over me: seared skin, cracked bones, pulled muscles torn from mangled joints. I tried to scream, but collapsed into hacking coughs as one lung fought to overcome its punctured partner.

I struggled to breathe, to move. I could feel the lagoon's waters pulling me forward, carrying me down. I blinked hard, clearing my vision, and stared at the blast crater I'd been washed into along with loose chunks of sand and earth. Something else swirled in the water around me: the gruesome evidence of death. A scrap of cowhide, a red slab of beef, two bright pink bird bodies, and a single white feather were all that was left of three poor animals.

As the wretched scraps flew into my pack, I clambered dizzily out of the crater. Dazed with shock, I stumbled back to the hill. Knees wobbled, thighs burned. I staggered over waves of pulsing pain. How could I outrun more of those creeping bombs? I glanced behind me, tripped, and crashed into the hard, bruising mass of a tree. The impact sent shock waves radiating through my injuries. Cracked lips opened for another scream, and this time they succeeded.

A long, deep, anguished howl exploded from both, not one, of my newly regenerating lungs. I was hyper-healing!

As walking became running, which became an all-out sprint, I could feel the bones fusing, the veins sealing. I could see my skin knitting together over rapidly rejuvenating tissue.

By the time I slammed the hut's door behind me, my broken body was nearly fixed.

Nearly.

With injuries still crying for help, I felt my hyper-healing peter out.

Food!

I reached into my backpack for some apples. Only one left,

along with the animal remains. I scarfed down the apple, but it barely made a dent. Next, I reached for one of the whole chickens, and devoured it without pause or thought.

Had anyone ever warned me about the dangers of eating raw poultry? Even if they had, would it have made any difference now? I couldn't think of anything beyond health. I was too desperate to stop the pain.

As soon as I swallowed the last bite of cold, rubbery meat, an eruption of nausea rose up from my churning stomach. I retched. I gagged. I could even see green bubbles floating up across my tearing eyes. I ran out onto the beach, trying to vomit out the infected muck.

But the world wouldn't let me. For a horrible, dry-heaving eternity, I had to just stand there and take it.

And if being assaulted by my own digestive tract wasn't bad enough, I found that the whole ordeal had barely helped me heal. "Insult to injury," I groaned.

Still gagging from the memory, I sourly peeked into my pack. "Okay," I told the rest of the animal parts. "I get it. You need to be cooked."

Making fire had just gone from a possibility to a priority, but, as I mentioned before, I still had no idea how to do it. Wracking my brain for some remembered hint, I came up with the notion of rubbing two sticks together. *If food poisoning can carry over to this world*, I reasoned, *why not this?*

Why? Well, for starters, I couldn't even put two sticks in my hands. I could hold one in the right, but not in the left. Anytime I put something in my left hand, it immediately went into one of the four small crafting corners.

"Great," I huffed, then tried to keep going with one stick.

All I ended up burning was time.

I couldn't rub the stick against anything. All I could do was hit. At one point I smashed a block of dirt out of the hut's wall, letting in a lot more light, but also reminding me that the day was now halfway done. After resealing the hole with more dirt, I tried my last option: hitting the stick against a plank of wood. "Ugh," I snorted as my stomach growled and my wounds seethed.

Like it or not, I'd have to take my chances with raw food. Passing over the other chicken, I warily eyed the steak. Was all uncooked meat unsafe or just the kind with feathers? *What I wouldn't give at this moment*, I thought, *for a licensed food safety inspector.*

I lifted the meat up to my face, sniffing it like a dog. I tried to picture what beef had looked like in my world, under glass in bright, chilly supermarkets, or steaming on a plate with veggies and mashed potatoes. I thought I recalled that the inside of that steaming steak in my mind was still pink, which had to mean it wasn't cooked all the way through.

That image caused another, powerful feeling to rise up from deep in my gut. It wasn't nausea this time, it was sadness. Without meaning to, I'd reminded myself of how little I knew about myself.

Why couldn't I picture anything past that steak on the plate? The table? The room? The faces of other people enjoying their dinner? Was I eating with my parents? My children? My friends? Was I eating all alone, like right now?

This line of thinking was leading down a deep dark hole, and so for sanity's sake, I pulled my mind back to the here and now.

"Okay," I told the slab of dead cow. "Please don't make me wanna puke, okay?"

I won't say the beef was *better* than the chicken; maybe a little tougher, with a rougher texture on the tongue. And it did have a tad more flavor. But what really mattered, of course, was that I didn't get sick, and all of my wounds finished healing.

I still couldn't believe this new superpower. Had I really almost been blown to bits barely a few minutes ago? How long would it have taken my world's medicine to put the pieces back together? Hours in surgery, weeks in intensive care, and months—maybe even years—of physical therapy. Not to mention all the necessary resources, the bandages and casts and space-age machines, and the army of trained professionals to apply all those resources. And what about the money to pay those professionals? And what if I hadn't had that money?

Even my painted-on clothes had miraculously sewn themselves back together. Looking down at my self-repaired shoes reminded me of a story of a man who had no shoes realizing how lucky he was when he saw a man with no feet.

"Be grateful for what you have," I said, nodding to my restored limbs.

GRRRP, growled my empty stomach, reminding me that while I might be whole again, I was now mightily hungry.

"You'll just have to wait," I said, turning my nose up at the chicken and its egg—which, by the way, had somehow gone through the explosion without so much as a crack.

The seeds, which had caused this whole near-death experience, had also survived the creeper attack. I planted them in a row behind my first cultivated square, all the while hoping this wasn't a giant waste of time.

As the last of the shoots rose from the cultivated earth, a sudden chill ran across my back. I looked up to see the sun just beginning to dip below the western edge of Disappointment Hill. *One of these days*, I thought, heading for the hut, *I gotta figure out how long these days are.*

I shivered again in the afternoon shade, confused at the sudden chill. Was the season changing? Had I not noticed the temperature drop at night? Neither of these hypotheses turned out to be true, but it'd be a while before I understood that I was suffering from the initial symptoms of starvation.

For a moment I considered climbing the hill to soak up some warming rays. From there, I might spot a few more elusive apple trees.

Another rippling shiver held me back, though, and this one

came from fear. I'd been caught out in the open twice already. Not again. Tonight I'd get indoors well before the monsters came prowling. Today had driven home the need for a bomb-proof bunker. *And I thought this was gonna be such a good day,* I thought, shuffling gloomily back to my shack.

The light outside my door was just turning purple by the time I smashed out several more blocks of cobblestone. As on the previous evening, the darkness of the cave made for slow going. I knew in my head that darkness alone couldn't hurt me. But try telling that to my heart. This fear wasn't rational. It was primal.

At one point I thought about knocking out a square in the hut's wooden roof to let in a patch of moonlight. Then I pictured that patch darkening with a zombie or creeper literally dropping in. *Keep going,* I told my picking arms. *Dig it deeper, stronger, safer.*

While I made some decent progress, the monotony of mining allowed my mind to wander. The empty darkness filled with shapeless threats.

I could feel the jitters taking over, and at this rate I'd be in full meltdown before dawn. "Take a break," I finally said, "do some crafting, see if you can come up with some kind of weapon." I laid two sticks in the center of my crafting table, and tried a few cobblestone combos. The now familiar shovel hovered before me, then the hoe, then the pickaxe. But then, after arranging three blocks in an L around the top of my sticks, I saw the image of an axe.

"Two in one," I nodded, snatching the weapon from the air. "Maybe you'll work on a tree *and* a zombie's neck."

It felt good to know I now had something to defend myself with, but even better to know that keeping my mind occupied was the best defense against the shakes.

And so I kept crafting instead of digging, and was soon very glad I did. I tried messing around with nothing but cobblestone, seeing if I could make a bombproof-rock version of my door. What I got, instead, was a plain gray box with two vertical slots in the front.

I figured it had to be another crafting aid, maybe an "instant upgrader" to make older tools into better ones. I placed a cobblestone in the upper slot and my old wooden pickaxe underneath it. Suddenly, the tool vanished in a blaze of orange and yellow flames. "Fi . . . !" I began, before bumping my head again.

I laughed, did a jump-free happy dance, then leaned into the face-warming glow.

"Fire."

This was the final piece in the holy trinity of human evolution. Tool making, agriculture, and now a little piece of the sun! This is what had saved our ancestors from the coldest winters, what had protected them from the fiercest predators. I pictured a group of hairy, filthy, grateful cave dwellers huddled around its comforting glow, warming their hands and cooking their food.

Cooking!

This new device was a furnace, the bottom slot for fuel and the top for whatever needed heating. Sure enough, the cobblestone I'd put in the upper slot had now fused back into a solid monolith.

As the fire died, I reached carefully for the block, ready to drop it before I burned my hand. It didn't. No need. One more quirk of this world was that items cooled the second they left the furnace. "Now for the big test," I said, popping the last raw chicken into the top slot with a fresh plank of wood underneath. Once again, and without any means of ignition, the flames roared to life. The little shelter filled with the sounds and smells of popping grease. I grabbed the fully cooked bird even before the last of the fire burnt itself out. "Mmm," I moaned between salty, moist mouthfuls. "Mmm-mmm-mmm."

Light, heat, and now cooked food. "You know," I said, tossing a few more planks into the furnace, "this turned out to be a really good day."

CHAPTER 6

OVERCONFIDENCE

The chicken was delectable, but it wasn't completely filling. "Your turn," I told the egg, to which the egg could have answered "that's what you think."

Ever heard that expression, "You can't make an omelet without breaking a few eggs?" Well, here's this world's version: "You can't make an omelet."

You can't fit the egg into the furnace. You can't crack it into a bowl. You can't even step on it; so much for walking on eggshells. As a last resort, I tried tossing it in the air to hit it with a stick. But before I could swing, the incredible, inedible egg flew across the room, hit the wall, and disintegrated like a clump of tall grass.

"Great," I grumbled, just as my fire winked out.

Darkness returned, along with all my irrational fears. Peering into the furnace's lower slot, I saw I still had a few more untouched planks of wood. Why weren't they burning? Did the furnace only work when it had something to heat? Shivering with cold and nerves, I rifled through my belt and pack for something else to burn. The first thing I grabbed happened to be a block of sand.

Thankfully, the furnace accepted my offering, giving me light, heat, and a few seconds later, a whole new modern convenience. I should have known what I was making. Back in my world, it was everywhere; every building, every home, every vehicle, even over people's eyes to help them see better. It was one of the most vital components of human civilization and I'd had no idea how it was made. Not until I pulled the smooth, clear block from the furnace did I realize that heating sand got you glass.

"Dolt," I murmured, punching out a hole in the wall and replacing it with the transparent cube. "Did you ever ask where anything comes from?"

What an amazing thing a window is. It gives you the freedom to see the outside world, but the security of knowing that world couldn't come in. At least, that's what I hoped. In zombie stories back home, didn't people always board up the windows at the first sight of the living dead? Would I have to do that when my own cuboid corpses showed up?

For now, I couldn't hear any ghouls, and I couldn't see any through my new, south-facing window.

That's when I realized I'd placed it on the wrong side. My garden, the only thing worth looking at, was north of my hut. I started punching the glass, expecting it to pop out and hover like all the other blocks. Instead, it shattered like the egg.

"Oops," I said. "No problem, I got a whole beach worth of sand right outside." If I'd been more cautious or timid, or even just a little more patient, I might have made the smart choice and waited for the dawn.

But did I?

The night had gone so well. I'd been racking up so many wins. Fire, cooked food, and now glass for windows. For the first time since landing, I felt fully in control of my situation. I was becoming overconfident, and that's what got me into trouble.

I'll just make a torch, I thought, holding a stick up to the furnace. *Monsters gotta be afraid of fire.*

When the stick refused to catch, I should've taken it as a sign to stop and think.

But did I?

The glow from the cabin's gotta be enough to keep everything away, I reasoned, sauntering out to the moonlit shore. Shovel in hand, trying to whistle through my thin, flat lips, I couldn't wait to make all kinds of cocky mistakes.

And I made a ton.

Instead of digging right outside my door, I chose a spot halfway up the beach. Instead of gathering a few cubes and dashing back, I just kept going until I'd dug myself into a hole. Instead of keeping my eyes and ears open—long after the fire died in my cabin, I might add—I fantasized about all the cool things I could build with this glass. A skylight, or wraparound windows, or maybe even a greenhouse if I dug up enough sand.

"Sssp." A sharp, rasping hiss yanked me out of my nighttime daydream. I froze, looking up.

"Sssp!" came the sound again, gripping my gut with recalled terror. It was the same rasp I'd heard that first night in the forest, when I'd seen those terrible eyes.

And here they were again, passing right over me: a cluster of small glowing rubies embedded in a black, cow-sized, eight-legged beast.

Spider!

Before I could run, move, or think, it'd jumped into the hole with me. Snapping jaws tore at my chest. I toppled backward, dropping my shovel. The spider pounced. I dodged. It spun for another strike as I scrambled frantically out of the pit.

"Sssp!" Scratching legs behind me, coming up fast.

My axe . . . back in the cabin . . . too far!

"Sssp!" A bite on the leg . . . pain . . . fear . . .

I reached into my belt for something, anything . . . sand. Nothing but sand!

Maybe if I could lay a roof, if I could trap it underground . . . I reached the top, the spider at my heels. I turned, hit it with a block of sand, then placed that block at the hole's edge. But the sand didn't stick. It fell. "Ssssp!" hissed the predator as the tan cube crashed onto its head.

I placed another falling block, then another, and another. The spider hissed angrily, pinned under more and more debris. I didn't know if I was doing any harm, I just wanted to keep it buried long enough to escape. The spider rasped. I kept going. It flashed red. I kept going. The nightmare hunter gave one final, enraged hiss, then poofed away in a puff of white smoke.

For a moment I watched in disbelief, panting as my wounds healed, my stomach growled, and my brain absorbed a new realization: Too much confidence can be as dangerous as having none at all.

Vibrating with adrenaline, I looked hastily around for more creatures. Nothing stirred on the beach, hill, or sea. I rushed back down into the pit to get my shovel, and on the way out felt something hop into my pack. I didn't know what it was till I'd gotten safely back to my cabin and thrown the remaining sand blocks into the fire.

The spider had left me a going away present, a short, sticky string of silk. I examined the strand for a few seconds, trying to think of some use for it, when the last plank in the furnace burned out.

".Ah nuts," I griped, and reached into the storage chest for more wood. I noticed there weren't too many planks left, not compared to all the worthless saplings stored next to them. And then I hit on what I thought was a brilliant idea.

I slid the dozen or so green mini-trees into the furnace and they promptly blazed to life. *Way to stretch your resources*, I thought with a self-congratulatory smile. I thought I was being so clever. I had no idea I was creating nothing short of an environmental tragedy that would come back to haunt me later. That night, as the little green saplings crackled brightly, I couldn't have been more chuffed.

"Mission accomplished," I said, hoisting my stone-tipped pickaxe. The addition of light allowed me to start thinking about how I wanted the finished room to look. Given my height, and the space I'd need for modern conveniences—crafting table, storage chest, and furnace—I imagined a seven-by-seven-block area with a raised ceiling for hopping victory dances. And I felt like doing that dance tonight.

My emotional roller coaster took another dive, however, when the furnace fizzled after little more than a minute. "So soon?" I grumbled, seeing that the saplings were all gone. There'd been so many and they'd lasted maybe a third as long as wood. *Good riddance*, I thought, tossing in the rest of the planks.

I can cut down more trees tomorrow, I thought. *Right now what I need is light.*

The key word here was "need." I'd already started this evening with an overwhelming fear of the dark, but now, between the giant spider attack and my discovery of fire, I couldn't let the night back in.

What happened next was nothing short of a race; a tense, sweaty frenzy to keep my shelter illuminated. At first I thought I was doing all right, until the last of the sand melted into glass.

Cobblestone, I thought, going back to the first material I'd used to discover fire. I didn't care that the end result was the exact material I was now trying to clear away. It was the process that kept me warm and safe. But I'd only just gotten back to work when the last of the planks died out.

"More wood!" I hissed, looking over at the hut's plank-and-slab ceiling.

Hastily walling off the bunker from the shack, I started chopping up the latter's wooden roof. I tried not to think about what would happen if a creature found me so exposed. I needed more fuel, more light!

What I *really* needed was to snap out of my funk and remember the mantra about panic drowning thought, as well as a new one that applies to all the others: It's not wisdom that counts, but wisdom under pressure. Stoking the furnace's bottom slot, I rushed to pick more cobblestone for the top. I had to keep the balance going.

How much longer until dawn?

The last plank fizzled. I tore through my pack for something to burn. I threw in the trapdoors, regular doors, that thin, flat, pressure plate thing, even the little push button that didn't last more than a few seconds.

Then I started burning my tools. *Just the wooden ones*, I promised. *I don't need them anyway.* But once they were gone, I turned on the stone versions. In went the shovel, then the hoe, and finally the axe, all fed to the waning flames and my ever-growing mania.

Ironically it was that mania that kept me from throwing in the last two wooden items I had: a couple of standard sticks. Since my cracked, worn, stone-tipped pickaxe looked about ready to break, I thought I might need to make another one to collect more cobblestone for the furnace.

Whichever goes first, I thought, hammering at the bunker's back wall. *If the flames go first, I'll use the sticks. If the pickaxe snaps, then—*

The fire died. The darkness returned. But in that final second of fading light, as the last block of stone flew from the wall, I thought I could see something different behind it. Were black spots embedded in its face?

Blindly picking away, I heard the crack of a successful strike. But instead of the new rock flying into my pack, I got a small, hard, black lump.

It didn't feel familiar, not like the sense memory of that first dirt block I smelled. This was more distant, like I'd heard of this substance without ever having seen it up close.

Wasn't there a natural resource that my people had been pulling out of the ground for centuries? Hadn't it been controversial; dirty and dangerous, but also plentiful and cheap? Not oil. Oil was a liquid. This might be—

"Coal?" I asked the lump. "Are you coal?"

I placed it in the furnace's lower slot and stood back as it flared right up.

"Coal or not," I said with a grin, "I'll take it!"

By its guiding light, I rushed over to the original mining point and found an identical black-flecked block. Picking out the nodule, I hurried back to the furnace.

I didn't have to. The first coal fire kept burning, and burning, and burning! At this rate it would last at least five times as long as normal wood. *And all on its own without me having to strike a match.* That last thought gave me the idea to try to make another torch.

Luckily I still had those two sticks for making a backup pickaxe. I held one up to the furnace just like I'd done earlier in the night. Hopefully this brighter, hotter, coal-fueled blaze would be able to do what the milder wood fire couldn't.

Just like before, the stick wouldn't catch.

I'd run out of luck, but not ideas. Thinking about this world's rule of combining materials, I placed a stick in the center square of the crafting table with the second lump of coal above it.

"Here we go!" I chimed, as four large, match-shaped torches jumped into my hand. "Let there be light!"

Feeling like the smartest person in the world—which might actually be the case if this world had no other people—I bounced back over to the still-burning furnace and exultantly held a torch to the flames.

And, once again . . .

Well, you get it.

"Grrr," I growled, in a tone that would have made any zombie proud. "What's missing?"

I knew the torch had to work eventually. This world wouldn't have let me make it otherwise. Would it? I just had to find the missing part of the equation, some kind of igniter I'd not yet learned to craft.

"Or maybe it's not that I need a new device," I said, remembering my experience with the hoe. "Maybe it's how I'm using this one."

I thought, given how fire worked in my world, that maybe I hadn't given the torch time to catch. Just like with the sticks, I'd held it against the flames for only a few seconds. Maybe it needed a lot longer.

I tried, again, to lean the coal-tipped cudgel against the furnace, and this time I counted a full sixty seconds. *Maybe longer?* I wondered, but saw that I was running out of time. The flames were dying. I couldn't have more than another minute. I'd have to use that precious light to try to dig for more coal. Reaching for my pickaxe, I decided, just on the spur of the moment, to place the torch on the ground next to the furnace. Who knows, maybe there was still a chance that the radiating heat would do the trick. Slim, I know, but still better than it sitting in my belt.

The moment I set the torch down next to the flickering firebox, it sparked into brilliant incandescence.

"Wha . . ." I sputtered, reaching for the smoky little flame.

The torch went out the moment I grabbed it, and then reignited when I set it back down. "How?" I asked incredulously, picking it up and sticking it to a wall, which caused it to spark again. How could a torch spontaneously combust when set down, then switch on and off like a flashlight?

The only answer I had was sheer acceptance of the fact that just because the rules don't make sense to me doesn't mean that they don't make sense.

And this time I couldn't have been happier about it! Not only did these torches work anywhere I set them; not only did they extinguish the moment I put them away; not only did I not have to worry about burning myself 'cause they gave off no heat; by far their most welcome, spectacular, completely nonsensical trait was the ability to burn forever.

You heard me. Forever!

Forget physics, forget logic, for-ev-er! Long after the furnace went cold, I watched them continue to keep my bunker as bright as day. *Now this*, I thought with nothing short of awe, *is something I'm pretty sure even my own world doesn't have.*

It might have seemed that easy back home, just flicking on a light switch and going about your business, but flicking that switch meant a power plant somewhere was using up some kind of stored fuel. Even the renewable energy I remembered hearing about needed a natural source; sunlight or wind or waves. Not here. Not with these. Yes, I'd need more coal to make more torches, but once I did, they'd burn as long as the stars!

"No more darkness!" I sang. "No more night!" Doing my victory dance, I hopped and spun around my hideout. "No more darkness, no more night, no more terror, no more fri—"

I stopped at the bunker's door, blinking at the daylight now shining through.

"Ha!" I chuckled happily, realizing that my nightlong battle had lasted well into the day. I stepped outside into the walled courtyard of my half-demolished shack. Looking first at where my wooden door used to be, before I burned it in my craze, I squinted up at the rising sun. I hadn't noticed until that moment that this world let me look right at the sun without damaging my eyes. I couldn't help feeling like there was some kind of reason for it.

"Don't worry," I told the warm, welcome square. "I won't need you tonight."

I went back inside, punched a wall-mounted torch into my hand, and then carried it back outside.

"You can rest easy now," I said, holding the torch up to the sun. "I'm done being afraid of the dark."

CHAPTER 7

TAKE LIFE IN STEPS

Smiling up at the sun, my stomach brought me back down to earth. I wasn't too hungry yet, but now that I'd eaten all I had left, the search for food had to be today's goal.

The first seeds I planted were higher than the others; not by much, but enough for me to try harvesting them. People ate sprouts, right? Alfalfa sprouts, brussels sprouts, maybe there were some new kind of—

I didn't get to finish the thought. The second I touched the shoots, they turned right back into seeds.

All right, I thought, putting them back in the ground, *so they just need a little more time, no big deal. There still have to be more apple trees,* I reasoned, picking my way up the hill. *I just haven't looked hard enough.* I poked my head over the top, and came face-to-face with another giant spider.

"Gah!" I gasped, instinctively jumping back. Out of control, I toppled down the hill, bounced off a rock, heard a sickening SNAP, and landed hard on the sand below.

Pain shot up my leg as I hobbled back to the safety of my bunker. *This isn't right,* I thought, slamming the door behind me. *This is daytime.*

Peering through the door's opening, I waited for a flash of legs and eyes. They never came. I opened the door nervously, tried to look in all directions, then took a tentative step outside.

And that first step scared me worse than any spider. My ankle still hurt. My hyper-healing wasn't working.

Of course I should have expected this now that my stomach was empty, but to actually have it happen was terrifying. Worry rose up on a bubble of realization. I was just a mere mortal now. Any major injury, any accident or monster attack, could be the end. I tried putting weight on my injured leg. White-hot nails of pain jabbed through my ankle.

What was I going to do now, if I couldn't outrun the spider? Just one of those vicious bites would finish me. But if I stayed where I was, if I didn't eat, didn't heal, I'd end up just as dead.

Grabbing my battered, nearly broken pickaxe, and what little nerve I had left, I limped carefully out onto the beach.

Nothing stirred up on the hill. I listened for the arachnid's familiar hiss. Silence. This time, instead of climbing back up the cliff, I thought it might be safer to swim around it.

I paddled slowly past the southern slope, keeping my eyes fixed on the summit. I got halfway around the hill when I spied the tips of two black legs. I froze in place, treading water as slowly and quietly as I could. The spider crawled creepily into view, its cherry red sensors locked on me.

I swam backward, ready to make for open water. If that thing didn't swim, maybe I'd have a chance to double back to another part of the island. I got a few strokes away before I realized that the arachnid wasn't coming after me. For a moment, we remained frozen, silently trading stares. Clearly it saw me, so why wasn't it attacking?

Did the light blind it, or was it something to do with the day itself? Were spiders only hostile at night? We watched each other for another few seconds before the eight-legged horror just up and disappeared. No fire, no smoke. One second it was there and the next, gone.

I swam back to shore, my mind flooded with questions. Why had it disappeared without burning? Why hadn't it been dangerous in daylight? And why had it lasted in the daylight after all the zombies had burned?

Limping back up onto the southern beach, I wondered if creepers also lasted longer than zombies, and if that was the reason I'd nearly been killed by one. I scanned the dense line of trees, making sure one of them wasn't a mottled green. I didn't see any creepers, thankfully, but noticed how dark the shaded wood was. Had the creeper been sheltering from the sun?

If that was true, and if there were other monsters hiding under those leaves, then that'd be the last place I looked for food. I limped west along the southern shoreline, looking for shellfish or even seaweed. The beach was completely barren. For the first time I also noticed that I hadn't seen any fish, or whales, or seals, or anything aquatic besides that sinister squid.

Coming around the edge of the island's southern claw, I saw that the water of the lagoon was as lifeless as the open sea. Squishing across its soft clay bottom, I climbed up onto the northern claw, looked down the beach, and spied a plant I'd never seen before.

It had stalks, three actually, that were light green and tall and growing right out of the seaside sand. "Bamboo!" I exclaimed, hopping painfully over. People ate bamboo, right? Wasn't it on some menus as bamboo shoots? If this was the mature version, then I could surely find a way to replant it and eat the shoots.

I took one swipe at the lowest section, and, unlike trees, the whole stalk came tumbling down. Collecting the three sections in my left hand, I saw the image of a grainy white pile in my right.

"Sugar," I said happily. "This isn't bamboo. It's sugarcane."

After so many failed attempts with the egg, I should have at least half-expected that this new food didn't want to be eaten. "Fine, whatever," I pouted, stuffing the pile and the two remaining stalks into my pack. "Bad for my teeth anyway."

Trying to stay positive, I wondered if the sugar might still be useful when combined with another ingredient—but what? I couldn't see anything else that remotely reminded me of food. No berry bushes, no mushrooms. There weren't even any worms or bugs, and believe me, in the state I was in, I would have gladly munched them down.

I even tried nibbling a few of the red and yellow flowers growing at the edge of the woods. Not only did they not oblige, but holding them in my left hand gave me the option of turning them into useless dye. "What else can go wrong," I grumbled, just as it began to rain.

"Had to ask," I moped, the warm, light drizzle perfectly matching my mood.

Limping tensely through the forest, my eyes flicked this way and that. I tried to keep my attention on the trees themselves and not what might be lurking behind them. It didn't help when I passed the crater that had almost been my grave.

Strangely enough, it hadn't yet filled up with water, even though a steady stream was flowing in. "Even the water here is weird," I muttered, and moved on to try to find an apple tree.

Which I didn't. The only trees left growing on the island had muted leaves and black and white bark which kinda reminded me of birches. I couldn't find one single apple tree, which I now called "oaks" because I didn't want to think of apples anymore. I'd always taken for granted that there had to be at least one more oak tree nestled somewhere in the forest. I figured, hoped, that I just wasn't looking hard enough.

Now I'd run out of excuses, and there was nowhere left to go but forward. *Maybe these birches also have fruit,* I wondered, grasping at straws—which, by the way, I also would have tried to eat. *Maybe they've got nuts or acorns or . . . something.*

With growing desperation, I punched out a few blocks of the nearest tree, whipped up a crafting table, and then a stone axe. I laid into the birches around me like a madman, swinging at trunks and leaves.

Nothing came down except more logs and a white-flecked sapling. "It's okay," I said, trying to stay cool. "Maybe this species just has fewer nuts. That's all, just gotta keep looking."

Pocketing the logs, I placed the useless sapling on the ground, and gave a startled shout as it suddenly grew up right in front of me. Chopping down that one turned out to be fruitless as well.

"Maybe this one," I grunted, turning to the next birch, "or maybe this one." Frustration growing into fear, I cut my way through the forest. "This one," I huffed, getting halfway through another tree before my axe snapped. Twisting back to my crafting table, I forgot about the injured leg.

Agonizing sparks erupted from my ankle. I slumped against

the half-cut tree, choking back tears, waiting for the throbbing to cease. I could deal with the injury but not with the pain. How could anybody? Feeling this way every minute of every day? How would you not go crazy? Isn't that why my world had whole shelves of different pain pills? Even if you weren't better, at least you felt that way, and right now that's all I wanted.

"Make it stop," I whispered. "Please. Please just make it stop."

"Cluckcluckcluck," came the sound of an approaching chicken.

"Get outta here," I barked, waving the annoying bird away.

The chicken looked up at me for a second, laid another unbreakable egg, then stubbornly pecked the grass at my feet. "Beat it!" I growled, waving my hands right in front of its face. I didn't need this right now, didn't need to see another creature eat, didn't need to be reminded of how delicious cooked chicken tasted.

"C'mon, now, I mean it!" I commanded, shuffling over to my crafting table. And it continued to follow me, pecking away while its clucking rang in my ears.

"Go!" I shouted, my fist clocking it in the beak.

"B'gack!" bawked the bird, sprinting away in a flash of red. "I didn't mean . . ." I started, guilt quickly replacing anger.

"Moo," came a friendly sound to my right. I looked over at the familiar eyes of the cow. In those eyes, in that serene face, I found the centering I needed.

"I know," I sighed. "I gotta get ahold of myself."

"Moo," it agreed.

"I gotta remember," I continued, "that no one's ever died of a twisted ankle, and if the sprouts grow into food then they'll take care of that."

Again, the cow gave an agreeable "Moo."

I could feel myself calming down, my breathing returning to normal. "Here I am acting like I did that first day when, well, look at all the progress I've made since then. I gotta remember that progress, and that vow I made to you the day I almost got lost at sea."

"Moo," said the cow, which prompted a quick correction.

"Okay, maybe it wasn't you, maybe it was your friend I was talking to who got killed by the creeper . . . and I'm sorry about the steak thing, by the way, but, you know, I was hungry and it was already dead and . . . well anyway, back to the vow."

I started pacing again, just like I had that first day with the cow, albeit with a pronounced shuffle. "I told myself that I had to figure out all the rules of this world, but I get now that I've gotta go further. I've gotta figure out rules for myself."

"Moo?" asked my bovine foil.

"No, I don't just mean the lessons I've been learning," I said, "or having a grand strategy like we talked about. I need a methodical way to achieve that strategy, a detailed discipline of specific steps for each individual task."

I stopped and turned on my good heel. "I know that's a lot of big words but what they boil down to is that I need to know not just what I have to do, but *how* I'm going to do it."

"Moo," chimed the cow, finally getting what I was saying.

"Isn't that what gets people through life back in my world?" I asked. "They get up every day and already know how they're going to face that day. That's what I need."

As the cow took a quick grass break, I kept pontificating.

"And I need to start with our strategy. Cover the basics, right? Food, shelter, safety. So, I got shelter, and food, well . . . I just figured out that there's nothing left to eat on this island other than sprouts which need time to grow. But safety?" I held up my wounded foot. "The whole reason I'm all panicked about food is because I can't hyper-heal anymore, but I wouldn't need to if I knew more about the creatures that can hurt me."

"Moo," said the cow, which I took for "Okay, I'm with you, but what does that have to do with your new method?"

"I'm getting to that," I said. "If I can study the creatures from a safe place and figure out where they come from, how they hunt, and how long they last when the sun comes up, I can keep out of trouble long enough to get a handle on food."

At that moment the rain ceased. I looked up at the sun, then down to the hill, then back over to the cow. "I've discovered how to make glass, so what if I built another room into this side of the hill to safely study the creatures, and *that*"—I held up a triumphant fist—"is where the method, or the 'way,' comes into play."

"Baa," said the white sheep, ambling over to us.

"Will you explain it to him?" I asked the cow, limping back toward the hill. Behind me, I could hear the sheep's confused "baa" and the cow's exasperated "moo."

"Take it in steps," I shouted over my shoulder. "I gotta take life in steps."

CHAPTER 8

THE WAY

I was thinking of crafting items in this world, how the process could be mental as well as physical.

By the time I'd swum back around to my beach, three clear steps had crystalized.

> PLAN: What do I want to do, right down to the smallest detail?

> PREPARE: What do I need—tools and materials— in order to make my plan work?

PRIORITIZE: What do I need to do *first* in order to do everything else?

This "way" guided my process in the creation of something I would soon dub my "observation room."

In my initial plan, I imagined a small chamber at the base of the hill's western slope, with an outer wall of glass blocks.

In order to create this room, I would need to prepare the following: glass blocks, torches, and extra tools.

Priority One was tools. Digging through the entire hill would take one, maybe two, extra pickaxes, which would take cobblestone and wood, which I had plenty of. Now that I was prepared with all the tools and materials I needed, and I had a mental plan of what I needed to build, I got right to work picking at the back wall of my bunker. At first things were going great. I almost forgot both my empty stomach and my aching ankle, until the deepening tunnel got darker.

How big is this hill, I thought, sticking a flickering torch to the wall. *What if I run out of torches?*

"If that happens," I said aloud, "then I'll just go digging for more coal and finish the observation room later." It felt good, for once, to have an answer instead of just worrying questions, to act instead of just react. Maybe this really was the way.

Turns out I didn't need more torches just yet. It wasn't long before I broke through onto the other side, and saw that the sun was dipping below the horizon.

"See!" I shouted over to the cow and sheep. "The way is working!"

"Baa," said the white sheep, reminding me that in less than a minute I'd be caught out in the open, in the darkness.

"Right," I said, placing my glass blocks. *Should have factored in the sunset,* I thought angrily, *and the size of the hill. Stupid planning, stupid mistakes.*

The cow must have known what I was thinking because it gave me an encouraging "moo."

"Good point," I called back. "This *is* my first time practicing the Three P's, which, now that I say it, means I should add a fourth: Practice!"

As the sun sank and the stars rose, I hollowed out a three-by-three-by-three chamber behind my new clear wall. All that was left was to fix my last, comforting torch to the wall.

"Not bad," I said proudly, wishing this world would let me rest my hands on my hips.

I turned back to the giant window, staring out at the twilight. So far nothing moved except the animals. "Well, at least I'm learning that you never stop eating," I told them. "Now, if only the monsters would show up."

"Add another P," mooed the cow. "Patience."

"Can't argue with that," I said, and settled down for a long wait.

The first thing I learned that night was that monsters didn't appear until the sky was completely dark. The next thing was that they literally appeared. They didn't crawl out of the ocean or the ground, like I'd initially thought. One second they weren't there, then the next, PLING! Okay, maybe I added the PLING! for dramatic effect, but you get it, right? They just materialized, and they didn't do it one at a time. They came in mobs, zombies and spiders and even those sneaky, combustible creepers.

I noticed that they didn't care about any of the animals, even when one of the sheep walked right in front of a zombie.

That zombie saw me, though, and made a beeline across the meadow. Instinctively I backed away into the tunnel. *Gotta build a door for this*, I thought, ready to slam down a couple cobblestones in the entrance.

The undead brute skulked slowly from one end of the window to the other, never taking its black eyes off me. Feeling a little emboldened by its passivity, I took a step forward, then another, then hobbled right up to the glass.

"Well?" I asked. "You gonna attack or what?"

Fittingly, I got a less than eloquent "Grrruuugggh."

"I know you can see me, and your buddy kept trying to break down my door, so what's the difference now?"

"Grugh," it growled grumpily, content to trade looks instead of blows.

"Well, at least I can't smell you," I sneered, but then added, "Can you smell me?"

The ghoul moaned, standing like a statue of rotten meat.

"Is that it?" I asked, pressing my face to the glass. "Is it 'cause you can't smell me?"

I had no way to test this theory, other than breaking a hole in the glass—which I was *not* willing to do—so I chalked it up, once again, to the rules making sense, just not to me.

Whatever the rule was—smell or maybe sound, or even some other, sixth sense I wasn't aware of—all the other mobs seemed to obey it, too.

Several of the spiders came skittering toward me, their eyes sending chills down my spine. One of the arthropods just sat there looking at me while another scuffled right over my window and up the hill. Like the zombie, neither seemed to have any interest in attacking.

Next came one of those silently gliding creepers, and this time I backed way up into the tunnel. If I was wrong about my sense theory, and if that living land mine decided to detonate next to the glass, I was toast. I even placed one block in the tunnel's entrance, and was ready to plant a second if I saw the creeper start to vibrate. Fortunately, block in hand, I watched the monster glide away.

My sigh of relief, however, was cut short the moment I saw another creature emerge from the woods. Like the zombie, this one was humanoid. However, unlike the putrid, stumbling flesh-bags, this thing had no flesh on its bones. In fact, it was only bones. It was a human skeleton, and the CLICKETY-CLACK sound it made matched what I'd heard that first night in the woods. "Was it one of you guys that shot that arrow?" I whispered.

I got my answer a second later when I noticed that the skeleton had something in his hand: a curved stick, or collection of sticks, tied together on either end by a taut string. "A bow. Mystery solved."

Just then another skeleton clacked into view and for a second I worried about the two of them taking pot shots at my window. Worry vanished when, to my astonishment, the two bone-beasts looked at each other, raised their bows, and began shooting! With each impact, the wounded skeleton was knocked back, flashing red, then returned fire.

"Oh I so gotta get one of those bows," I said, giddy with the idea of a ranged weapon. "Please just kill each other so I can grab one in the morning."

And then, as a teasing answer to my prayers, the skeleton battle was over. The new challenger had beaten his rival, shooting him into a cloud of smoke. I saw a bow hovering where the loser had vanished.

Patience, I reminded myself, watching helplessly as the bow hovered just a few dozen blocks from me. Glancing down the tunnel, I thought I saw the sky lightening through my door. "Won't be long now," I said, looking back at the prize. And then, to my utter anguish, the weapon blinked out of existence.

"No!" I whined, realizing that dropped objects in this world apparently have a lifespan.

I did pick up something that morning though: vital proof that my shade theory was correct. Watching two zombies, one in the meadow and the other in the woods, I saw the exposed one burst into flames, while the other remained safe.

While this was happening, I thought I heard a rapid clicking above my head. Was a skeleton running, or dying, somewhere up the hill? Maybe I'd get lucky and snag a bow after all! I waited until the CLICK-CLACKING ceased, then limped back to the tunnel.

I grunted and groaned with every smarting step up the cliff wall. In a replay of the previous morning, I got to the summit and into another staring contest with a spider.

"Okay," I said to the daytime nightmare, "If I'm right, then daylight makes you passive, and I'd really like to be right right now."

I could see something hovering behind its bulbous body. A bow?

"Good spider," I said, taking a cautious step toward it. "Good giant, carnivorous mutant." It stayed still. I took another. It looked away. I crept right past the arachnid and right over to the prize I'd literally risked life and limb for.

Not a bow, but the next best thing. The shaft was wood—oak or birch I couldn't tell—and the sharp, triangular tip looked a lot like flint. The end was made of a feather, which I guessed helped it fly straight. *So this is an arrow*, I thought. *Now if I can only get the thing to shoot it with.*

"Moo," came a call from down in the meadow.

"Yeah, I got it," I called back, holding up the arrow triumphantly. "But I also got reams of intel on those creatures of the night."

Mentally I ran through everything I'd learned from just one observation: how shade worked, how skeletons attacked each other, how nothing attacked me as long as I was safe behind glass. And that last observation brought up a lingering question.

"Why did they stay away? Was it the absence of smell or . . . or the light?"

"Moo," replied the cow, going back to its breakfast of green squares.

"Is it the light?" I pressed. "It makes more sense than smell, right? I mean, if sunlight kills monsters or"—I glanced sideways just in time to see the spider vanish—"banishes them, whatever you want to call it, then does a less powerful light, like a torch, keep them away?"

"Moo," called the cow over its black and white butt.

"I know," I said. "Only one way to find out."

Hiking down the easier but still painful western slope, I continued to talk out my next project with the cow.

"What if," I began, "I set some torches outside near my observation bubble so I can see if they work?"

Planning.

"But," I continued, "in order to do that, I need to make more torches, and to do that, I need to get more coal."

Preparing.

"Which means the first thing I need to do is make sure I have enough pickaxes and maybe a shovel or two in case I hit dirt or sand."

Prioritizing.

"Which I already know how to do."

Practice.

"Moo," warned the cow, reminding me of the need for . . .

"I know," I griped, eager to start my new adventure. "Patience."

It turned out that practice was really what I needed because I had no experience with mining. Isn't that what it's technically called? Mining? Digging down into the earth for mineral resources? Well, whatever it's called, I didn't know how to do it.

For starters, as I cut a rough diagonal staircase down through solid rock, I realized that I'd left light out of my planning. This meant I had to hop back up the stairs, which killed my ankle, to grab the torch from my bunker, and to place it and replace it on the stone wall every few blocks I dug.

It was slow going, and at one point almost fatal. Digging down a few dozen blocks, I came to a hard tan stone directly in front of me. Because the stone looked like sand, I dubbed it sandstone, and when I dug it out, an actual block of sand fell down to replace it. I got out my shovel and removed the new sand block, then the next sand block that fell in its place, then the third that fell in its place, then backed up as a stream of deep blue water rushed in.

I've broken through to the sea, I thought, shaking my head at the blunder. I hadn't thought about the fact that this island was essentially an underwater mountain, and digging at an angle would eventually find me out in the ocean.

At least this world's water is weird, I thought, remembering how the blast crater had never filled up. In my world, breaking into the sea would have flooded the entire tunnel, at worst drowning me and at best destroying all my work.

"I got that going for me," I said, turning around and digging in the opposite direction. "I don't have to worry about drowning." And then, looking up at the solid blocks above me, I said, "Or cave-ins."

I shouldn't have said that out loud. Yes, I thought I knew that sand was the only substance that didn't stick and that if I saw another sandstone block, I'd be well warned. And yes, I know that superstition and tempting fate are silly and primitive and wrong. Still, I shouldn't have said it out loud.

Because the next moment I knocked away a stone above my head and looked up just in time to see the block above it come crashing down.

The world went dark. I choked and gasped. I was drowning. Not in water, but in this hard, gritty stuff that scratched and crackled as I tried to struggle free. My hand burst into open air. I clawed at the smooth stone. Half crawling, half swimming, I wriggled out of the suffocating trap.

I stood panting on the last step of my tunnel, feeling like an elephant had sat on my chest. Bruised ribs, scraped skin, throat scratching like it was made of sandpaper. Looking up, I saw why. I'd just discovered this world's other nonstick substance, a material halfway between sand and rock.

Something I'd barely noticed in my world, maybe on somebody's driveway, had almost accomplished what zombies and giant spiders and creeping explosives had failed to do. "Gravel," I hacked, feeling the stinging wounds I'd now have to live with for who knows how long.

Getting out my shovel, I tried to clear the column away, and just like the sand, it kept filling in. Clearing the fourth cube, however, got me a little added bonus: another sharp flake of flint. Peering up into the hole above my head, I saw a huge deposit of gravel which might hold more flint flakes if I ever needed them.

"For now," I said softly, fearing my own voice might cause another cave-in, "I think I'll stay well away from you."

Changing the planning section of my way, I decided to modify my mining technique. Instead of going diagonally, I tried digging in a spiral: two blocks down, turn right, two blocks down, turn right, and so on. That way I not only avoided the ocean but also knew exactly what was above my head.

I might have been safer, but after being buried alive, I sure didn't feel it. I don't think I was claustrophobic at this point, but digging through these narrow confines of rock, with barely enough room above my head and only one torch that I had to keep hopping painfully back up my makeshift staircase to get, well, let's just say it wasn't my most pleasant experience.

At one point, when I probably should have been remembering the cow's warning about patience, I started to seriously consider giving up the whole operation. I began looking behind me more often, picturing the long, punishing climb back up. Was all of this worth it? Was my stupid experiment with torchlight and monsters just that? Heck, the whole point was to work on making myself safer, and I'd almost gotten myself killed. Maybe I should just forget—

A block of stone fell away from me to reveal flecks of black coal.

"Finally," I breathed in a chuckling groan. "About time you guys showed up." Picking out the precious black lumps, I added, "And there's so many of you, too." I counted at least a dozen of them, which meant forty-eight torches if I used all of them at once. *I can light a tree for my experiment,* I thought happily, *and my cave, and the observation room, and the tunnel, and make them all bright as . . .*

I stopped and stared at the rock behind the coal. It was speckled, but orange, and seemed to reflect the torchlight.

Some kind of metal? I wondered. *Copper? Brass?* Was brass a naturally occurring ore or was it a mixture of other elements? I still don't know the answer to that one.

I picked out the rock, and the two identical ones behind it, and unlike the coal, whatever was embedded in them stayed put.

"I think I know how to get you out," I said, hoofing it back up to the bunker and wincing with each painful step.

Making torches as I went, I made sure to place them far enough apart to light my entire way to the surface. You might say I was wasting the very material I'd come for, but if these three new cubes turned out to be what I thought they were, then I'd be going back down there soon.

I slid the three metal-flecked blocks into the furnace, placed a lump of coal beneath them, and watched as the fire blazed up. What came out wasn't copper or brass, but something much more valuable. What came out was nothing less than the metal that literally built the modern world. What came out was iron!

"Look!" I shouted through my observation bubble to the animals. Picking out a doorway next to my window, I hobbled across the meadow to show them the three shining bars. "Look what's right under our feet!"

"Moo," said the cow, with a chorus of "baas" from the two sheep and even a few distant "cluckcluckclucks" from the chickens.

"Yes, grass, ha-ha," I said, "but underneath that grass, underneath the dirt, stone, sand, and gravel is something that's going to change everything around here!" I raised the bars like an Olympic medal.

"'Cause thanks to my new method, the Way of the Five P's, I've just kicked the Stone Age into the Iron Age!"

CHAPTER 9

FRIENDS KEEP YOU SANE

"This is gonna be a good night," I boasted to the watching cow. "Not only do I have iron to work with, but"—I held up a handful of torches—"I'm also gonna prove that fire keeps the bad guys away."

After setting up twelve torches on the tree closest to the meadow, I waited behind my glass wall for the sun to set, the moon to rise, and for the monsters to make their appearance. And when they did, they walked right through my barrier of torchlight. Anger rising, temples throbbing, I uttered a very loud, very angry, very inappropriate word.

"Guhhh," gloated the first zombie who slouched up to my window.

"You win this one," I said, holding up the three iron bars, "but I'm just getting started."

Now, if you're already a veteran of this world, then you know what kind of weapon can be made with iron. The same one you can also make with stone or just wood, and the same one I couldn't imagine making at the time. I wasn't thinking clearly, okay? There were a lot of reasons for this: frustration, hunger, and one that I'll go into later because I wasn't aware of it yet.

For now, just know that I wasn't using my noggin the way I should have, and therefore all I could conceive of was an iron version of my axe. Which I didn't craft, by the way, because it would have taken up the only three precious ingots I had.

Conserve your resources, I thought. *Figure out what you* could *make, then only make what you need.*

As the night wore on, and one mob after another marched mockingly past my harmless torch tree, I stood at a crafting table in front of my glass wall, watching one ghostly item option after another pass me by.

The only two worth mentioning ended up becoming critical to my survival, even though I didn't know it at the time. The first one, which would have cost me two ingots, looked kind of like a pair of scissors but with the handles connected instead of crossed. I think the technical term is "shears." The other one, which would have cost me all three, was nothing more than an iron bucket.

"That's it?" I growled with exasperation. "A bucket and shears? That's the best I can do with iron?" The night had been a total washout—first the torches, now my supposed Iron Age. "And I had such high hopes," I said, sighing in a moment of deep self-pity.

I glanced up from the crafting table and saw a zombie in the meadow burst into flames. The sun's first rays were just poking over Disappointment Hill on what I now thought of as Disappointment Morning.

"That's right!" I shouted through the glass. "Burn!" At least my enemies wouldn't live long enough to celebrate my night of failure. "Burn, burn, burn!" I chanted, and smelled a new, offensive odor: my own breath.

I haven't said much about bodily functions in this story so far, because, so far, I hadn't had any. No poo. No pee. None of the gross-but-necessary stuff I used to do back home. I hadn't even let off that musical gas that's got so many creative nicknames. Which I did *not* miss, by the way, given that I lived in a stuffy dugout with no ventilation!

But now, for some reason, I suddenly had the sour stink of morning breath, although I suspected it didn't have much to do with the morning.

My headache from last night hadn't gone away, either. If anything it had gotten worse. Chills were also rippling across my back, even though the room temperature hadn't changed. I realized how weak and listless I felt. Not tired, just lead bones and concrete muscles. At the same time, my heart knocked wildly against my chest.

"Am I starving?" I asked, smelling my own breath blow back at me from the window. "Is this how it feels?"

Of course it was, and I knew it. I'd lived with hunger since I'd gotten to this world, but in my heart of hearts I never really believed it would kill me. Accidents and monsters—immediate, in-your-face hazards—were real, but slowly wasting away?

I don't think I'd ever been close to that kind of danger in my old life. Lethal hunger was for other people, old people reminiscing about wars and depressions, or far-off, nameless strangers begging for aid on TV.

Now I understood them. My body, like a machine, had run out of fuel, and it was breaking down. How long did I have before the machine broke entirely?

"Moo," came a distant call from across the meadow, reminding me of what I had to do.

"The garden!" I exclaimed, waving gratefully at the cow. "Today's the day," I told myself with each limping step, "the shoots have to be ripe."

And they were. At least that's what I hoped. One of the cultivated squares had grown into tall, golden hanging stalks heavy with large, black, mini-cubed kernels of . . . what? Wheat? Barley? Rye?

Wheat, I thought, and reached out for the beckoning square. I not only came up with a collection of seeds, which I promptly replanted, but also a thick bushel of grain.

Lifting the bushel, my hand froze bare inches from my mouth.

"It's edible," I said, refusing to consider that the whole project was a blind alley. "I just need to do something with it."

Hobbling back to my bunker, I kept uttering, "Don't give up." And when the furnace refused to cook the grain, I added, "Panic drowns thought."

"Just gotta combine it with something," I muttered, throwing the bushel and anything else I could find onto the crafting table. "That's it, yeah, combine, that's what you do here, combine stuff."

And that's what I tried to do for half the day. Countless combinations of the egg, sugar, even flowers, wood, and dirt. I must have looked crazy, babbling to myself through one failed experiment after another. By the several-dozenth dud, I looked up and shouted, "More!"

That had to be the answer. One bushel wasn't enough. Just like multiple woodblocks or cobblestones, I just needed more wheat!

Limping back outside, praying that the morning had given

one more square a chance to ripen, I saw that the garden was still green.

I began to swear, then noticed something that'd completely slipped by me before. The square I'd harvested hadn't been the first one I'd planted, but rather the closest to the ocean.

"Water!" I cried, furious at my own stupidity. "Plants need it to grow!"

And yes, if I'd been in my right mind, I probably would have done what you're thinking of right now. I would have just dug a trench from the water's edge to let it run right past the rest of my crops.

But I didn't. Instead, my scared, starving, screwed-up brain devised the worst of all possible plans.

"The bucket!" I rasped, remembering what I could have crafted the night before. Now, using the beachside table, I whipped the three iron ingots into a metal pail. A second later, I'd scooped up a full, brimming load of water, and the second after that I poured it right onto the row of plants.

"NO!" I screamed as the stationary liquid cube washed not only the seeds, but all my work, energy, and time, out to sea. I dove in after them, snatching the hovering green pebbles from the shallow sand ledge. "Right back where I started," I whispered at the seeds. Then, in a mounting torrent of rage, erupted, "Right back where I started!"

Blinded by fury, I ran across the beach, punching anything

in front of me: sand, dirt, even the solid stone wall of the cliff, all to the roaring chorus of "Right! Back! Where! I! STARTED!" And on that last word I hurled the bucket into the ocean.

The act seemed to suck all the anger right out of me, replacing it with the clarity of consequences. I watched in horror as my brand new, extremely rare, and possibly useful pail sailed up and out into the blue.

"Oh no," I whispered, plunging back into the cold depths. Unlike the seeds, I'd thrown the bucket much farther out. I tried swimming underwater, looking in its general direction and seeing nothing but inky midnight. I splashed to the surface, inhaled deeply then crash-dived like a submarine.

There it was! In the purple haze of subsurface sunlight, I could just make out a small object hovering on a narrow ledge of gravel. Just one block over, and it would have been lost forever. I spluttered back up to the surface not only with the bucket, but with the knowledge that tantrums never help.

Trying to remain calm and digest this new lesson—the only thing I *could* digest—I began replanting my seeds. I scooped up the cube of water and was about to pour it back into the sea when I suddenly had the idea of drinking it. True, I'd never been thirsty, and true, water alone wouldn't stave off malnutrition, but at least a full belly might make me feel a little better.

Like with the wheat and so much else before it, my hand and mouth practiced passive resistance. I didn't get upset, though, and not just because I was hanging on to sanity by my square fingernails. The idea of drinking had set off another thin, wobbly, but possibly lifesaving train of thought.

"Can I drink anything else?" I asked the now empty bucket, and with impeccable timing, I heard a distant "moo."

Milk!

Shaking my head, I limped back to the observation bubble. "How could I forget this?" I asked the blotchy, grazing mammal on the other side of the glass. "Even if I didn't drink milk at home, even if I was lactose intolerant, I still should have remembered where milk came from."

The cow snorted, probably saying, "Took ya long enough."

I walked outside and circled the animal a few times. "How do you . . ." I began awkwardly. "I mean, what's the right way to . . ."

Clearly I'd neither milked a cow or ever seen it done in my world. However, a quick, terse "moo!" reminded me that the complexity of tasks in that other world didn't apply here.

"Right," I said, holding the bucket out to its—her?—pinkish udder. "I'll be as gentle as I . . ." I started to explain, but before the thought was finished, the pail filled with creamy, frothy liquid.

"Thank you," I said, smelling the rich, familiar scent. I drank long and deep, savoring every drop. I waited for my stomach to fill, my wounds to heal, my worries to melt into a river of dairy bliss.

None of that happened. I didn't even feel the liquid in my belly. "I know," I said nervously, milking another pail and hobbling back into my observation room. "I just need to keep going!"

Feeling the demons rise, the panic and frustration and explosive, raging hopelessness, I leapt into combining this new ingredient with every other edible mixture I could think of.

Milk and egg, milk and wheat, milk and egg and wheat, milkeggwheatsugar . . . this and that, back and forth. "My last chance," I babbled incessantly, "last chance, last chance."

That chance evaporated as every possible combination failed.

"It doesn't . . ." I stammered, staring at what should have been all different kinds of food, "doesn't make sense."

Past lessons came flooding back, about things not having to make sense to me to make sense, and how I shouldn't assume anything that I couldn't prove. And that's when I remembered the proof of another kind of food, one I'd already eaten, and which was now standing right in front of me.

My brain switched off. It wasn't a tantrum, not this time. I wasn't hot-tempered now, but rather very, very cold.

I looked up from the crafting table into the meadow, out at the cow which had turned its back on me. My mouth filled with spit, my stomach with digestive juices. My body knew what it wanted. Images of steak filled my brain as the axe handle filled my hand.

I slouched slowly across the grass, breathing heavily in a cloud of my own foul breath. The cow didn't move, munching on its last meal, ignorant of my approach. I shuffled closer. It took no notice.

Just a few more steps, just a few more seconds, and it would all be over. The cow fed peacefully. I raised the axe.

Meat.

Food.

Life.

The cow turned and our eyes met.

"Moo."

I dropped the axe and staggered back.

"I . . . I'm sorry, my friend," I told the gentle beast. "Because you *are* my friend, even though I don't deserve you."

Soft, heaving sobs cut into every word. "You're—all—I—have."

And only then did I realize how truly lonely I was. I might not have remembered my life from the other world, and the other people I shared that life with, but I knew they had to exist. Friends, family—why else would my soul feel as empty as my stomach? Why else had I talked to myself, materials, monsters, even the sun up above?

I was trying to fight the isolation that was as deadly to my mind as starvation was to my body. Survival, I now understood, meant taking care of them both. That's why I'd always felt so comforted talking to the animals. No, they couldn't talk back, but they could feel, they could hurt, and they wanted to live just as much as I did. And sharing those basic needs meant I would never be alone.

"Friends keep you sane," I said, picking up the axe at my feet. "And if I'd used this, I'd have ended up just like a zombie."

"Moo," said the cow, trying to lighten the mood.

"You're right," I chuckled. "I guess I kinda look halfway there already." With my unhealed bruises, my limping stride, and my breath smelling like a garbage pile, I could see that my four-legged pal had a point. But was she just making a joke, or trying to get me to see something I'd missed?

Putting the axe in my belt, my eyes fell to the pouch next to it, the one containing the stacked, stinking piles of collected zombie flesh. "You know something, Moo," I said, abruptly naming the cow, "there is *one* potential food source I still haven't tried."

"Moo," agreed the pardoned filet mignon.

Just looking at the chunks of meat made me queasy. "Hopefully," I said, crafting a table, then a furnace, "I won't have a repeat of the raw chicken."

The spoiled flesh wouldn't cook. The furnace didn't want it any more than I did.

"Moo," insisted the cow, as I held the fetid hunk to my nose.

"What if it's worse than the chicken? Maybe I should wait and—"

"Moo!"

"All right!" I snapped, and popped the vile piece of carrion into my mouth. I chewed and gagged and swallowed and gagged a whole lot more.

I didn't get sick like with the chicken, but I almost wished I had. What happened to me was something new, something terrible, and something unique to this world.

Call it ravenousness, or hyper-hunger, but I suddenly wanted to eat the entire world. It felt like my stomach was trying to consume itself, as if every cell was a miniature mouth snapping and screaming for food. At the same time my mouth felt like I'd just licked the sludge off the bottom of a summertime Dumpster.

"Ghaaa," I gasped in what must have been a spot-on zombie impression. I coughed, I wretched, I ran in frantic circles, looking for anything to chase away the taste. I pressed my face to a tree, trying to actually lick the bark. I jumped into the lagoon, trying to force a drop of water between my lips.

"Moo!" Moo was trying to throw my taste buds a lifeline. *Milk!*

I still had the second helping from my failed experiments. I grabbed the bucket and chugged like there was no tomorrow. And then suddenly I was fine. Hyper-hunger: gone. "Thanks!" I gasped to Moo, climbing out of the lagoon and noticing that my ankle suddenly felt a little better.

I tried a few more steps and, while not entirely healed, the sharp pain had faded to a dull ache. I took a deep breath and, lo and behold, my bruised ribs felt better.

"This?" I asked Moo, holding up another chunk of gourmet ghoul. "*This* is the answer?"

Moo gave me an impatient snort, as if to say, "Don't think about it. Just do it!"

"Right," I said, milking her again and holding the bucket ready. It was almost worse the second time, because now I knew what was coming.

"Oy." I winced, and bit into the decaying grossosity.

I chewed, gulped, and chased with the second pail. This time the hyper-hunger barely lasted a second, and when it was done, my wounds were almost healed.

"Oh, that's better!" I breathed, feeling a little of my strength return.

"This doesn't make me a cannibal, right?" I asked, imagining the repulsive substance in my stomach. "I mean, if zombies just spawn as-is, then they couldn't have ever been human, right?"

"Moo," said my bovine buddy reminding me just to be grateful.

"Yeah, I know," I admitted. "At least I won't have to worry about starving. In fact, I think there's a saying where I come from: Don't live to eat, just eat to live."

I looked up at the setting sun, thinking of tonight's zombies in a whole new way. "Thank you," I told Moo, milking her for another pail, "not just for this, but for, you know, everything, even after what I almost did to you."

And then my generous, nurturing, unbelievably awesome pal gave me the third and final gift of friendship that day. "Moo," she said, which I knew meant, "I forgive you."

CHAPTER 10

NOTHING CLEARS THE MIND LIKE SLEEP

That night my stomach growled along with the undead vermin. Watching them spawn through the safety of my observation bubble, I actually found myself staring hungrily at the roving mobs, impatiently hoping for the dawn to turn them into bits of disgusting mush.

Now I'm a scavenger, I thought, clocking every zombie's spawn point. *Isn't that what they call something that survives on dead meat? A vulture or a hyena or a maggot, that's me.*

I thought I remembered hearing somewhere that early hu- mans had started out that way, chasing off other scavengers to feed on the picked-over carcasses of animals. Maybe it was true, or maybe I was just trying to make myself feel better.

At least it was easier to track the ghouls by the glow of my torchlit tree. *Maybe it wasn't a total waste after all,* I thought, not realizing how right I was. As the night wore on, I noticed that no zombies—or any mobs, for that matter—spawned anywhere near the circle of light. They materialized everywhere else; in the forest, the meadow, by the lagoon—even on the beaches, from what little coastline I could see—but never close to the luminous tree.

"Can mobs only spawn in darkness?" I asked myself, but got an unexpected answer from the back bunker door. Rotted fists were knocking loudly, accompanied by hostile groans.

"Delivery!" I called, walking back down the tunnel and over to the beachside exit. Sure enough, a zombie was pounding on the thin wooden barrier. "You just stay there," I said, marveling at how different this moment was from the first time a ghoul had tried to break in. "This'll be no different than ordering pizza."

I shouldn't have said that last word, because it reminded me of what real food tasted like. *Pizza . . . lo Mein . . . chicken tikka masala . . .* I don't know what my particular preferences were back home, but at that moment they all sounded good.

Lost in culinary memories, salivating at every dish my species had to offer, I heard the standard, high-pitched barks of a burning zombie. Dawn had broken, and the undead assailant was now seconds from death.

"If that ain't ironic," I told the smoldering somnambulist, "and here *you* were trying to eat *me*." A few seconds later, I was gagging down my decomposing breakfast.

Be grateful for what you have, I reminded myself through gulps of blessed milk. And I had a lot to be grateful for, because by the last swallow, I found my body completely healed. My bruises were gone, my headache faded, and my ankle took its full weight without any complaint. Even my breath smelled sweet and normal again, which was another irony if you think about the putrefaction it had just been filled with.

"Be grateful," I said, trying and failing to forget the memories of human cuisine.

Cheese enchiladas, French fries and ketchup, blueberry pancakes with maple syrup and a side of bacon . . .

"I gotta get some real food," I said, walking over to the little garden. No luck there. The new seedlings were barely a mini-cube higher than they'd been the day before.

"Ugh," I groaned, wincing at the memory of yesterday's disaster. Where would I be if I hadn't bungled it so badly? Would breakfast have been a bowl of wheat-based cereal instead of a mouthful of zombie-o's?

"Don't dwell on your mistakes," I said, forcing myself back to the present. "Learn from them."

And learn from them I did, because studying the garden

showed me that the seeds planted right next to the sea were growing faster than the others.

I was right! I thought excitedly. *I was right about water, just not about how to use it.*

"Don't put water *on* the seeds," I said, wishing I could smack my head, "bring it *next* to them!" It was so simple, so easy. Why hadn't I thought of it before?

Whipping out my shovel, I dug a trench alongside the seeds. Water came flowing in, but, in the bizarre physics of this world, didn't fill all the way up. I got out my bucket, scooped up a cube of seawater, and dumped it on the back of the ditch . . . and learned yet another quirky world rule. If you have two cubes of water and you put them three blocks apart, the space in between becomes an entirely new cube of water. And not just temporarily. You can take out that new cube, and the next one after it, and the next one after that until you've got enough to make a lake. Just two starter cubes can probably make a whole ocean. The point is, in this world, water makes water.

Why am I obsessing over this small, odd, boring little factoid? Because later on in this story, that little factoid will end up saving my life.

But back to the here and now.

Watching the trench fill to the top, I remembered a tale about an impatient amphibian trying his hand at gardening. In the spirit of that tale, I bellowed, "Seeds, start growing!"

Chuckling at my own wit, or, rather, quoting someone else's,

I still knew that I had to wait a bit to try combining wheat with wheat. And that was assuming, again, that this *was* wheat.

Patience, I told myself, trying not to think about how many more meals of zombie flesh I'd have to choke down. *Patience.*

Something splashed off to my right. I looked up and saw a squid.

"Ya know," I called out to the eight-armed sea monster, "there's another thing on this island, or, rather, swimming next to it, that I haven't tried to eat yet!"

I was feeling pretty confident by this point. I had my strength—and more important, my hyper-healing—back. I was jonesing for some new challenges, especially when the reward might be a decent-tasting meal.

Grabbing my axe, I shouted, "Calamari time!" and jumped into the water. Sensing what was coming, the squid began to jet away. "Yeah, that's right!" I called after it. "I used to be afraid of you, remember?"

My octo-prey stopped just below the surface, allowing me to take a swing. I stopped to raise my axe, and promptly sank. Silently laughing—yes, I'm sure it was laughing—my seafood lunch moved away.

"Come back!" I called, swimming after it again. "Get back here and get in my furnace!"

I followed the squid around the southern shore of the island, trying to swim and swing at the same time. In case you haven't realized yet, it can't be done. Just like this world wouldn't let me rub my head while patting my stomach, it wouldn't let me do anything while swimming except swim. I finally came to this realization after about five tragically comical minutes, which ended with the squid jetting into the deep.

"Don't say it," I said, floundering ashore and into the judgmental gaze of Moo. "I know I gotta make another boat." Which I did. I then used that boat to go after a whole group of squid, hacking at the water and getting myself all twisted around. I can't blame the rules of the world this time. Technically, I guess it's doable. For all I know you've done it yourself. But me? I'm just glad nobody was there to see how ridiculous I looked. Well, almost nobody.

"Moo!" called my cow critic from the beach.

"Yeah, well why don't you come out here and try it?" I called back, realizing a second later that she'd actually been trying to warn me. Looking up, I saw that not only was I getting farther and farther out to sea, but night was barely minutes away.

"Tomorrow," I promised Moo, gliding back to land. "I'll give it another try."

She just snorted back.

"No, I will!" I insisted, knowing that she was right. Stamping back to my observation bubble, I realized that the whole idea of boat fishing was over. I needed something else, another method or maybe an entirely different tool.

As the sun surrendered to the stars, I tried to think of some way to snag a squid. Ideas were hard to come by that night. I found my mind wandering, unable to stay on task. I drifted from memories of my time on the island to observations through the window, to hazy recollections of my past world. They weren't anything specific, just sense memories of my eyes burning, my fingers cramping, and my bottom going numb from too much sitting. What did it all mean? And why now? It was like some kind of fog had settled in my brain that I hadn't seen building until now.

"Gotta think," I said, wishing I could rub my temples.

That was when a skeleton clacked out of the woods, driving home how truly loopy I was getting.

"A bow!" I exclaimed, looking down at the arrow in my belt. "Why didn't I think of this before?"

I'd been so keen on recovering one for so long. Why had it slipped my mind until now? Fortunately, the skeleton had shown itself only a minute or so before dawn; and even more fortunately I recovered both its bow and another arrow.

"Now you'll see!" I boasted to Moo, who was breakfasting with the two sheep. "Baa," called the black sheep, which I named Flint.

"Right, thanks," I nodded. "Gotta practice."

And practice I did. Shooting countless times at the same tree, I spent the entire morning becoming a reasonably capable archer. I learned how high you had to aim the bow and how far you had to pull back the string to get the right range. By noon, I felt ready to test my skills out on a live target.

"You guys ready for this?" I asked my animal audience. "Witness the master at work!" As a vote of no confidence, they continued to graze with their backsides to me. "Just wait," I said, walking out to the beach. "One calamari entrée comin' right up!"

I spotted the closest squid about a dozen or so blocks out to sea, drew back the bowstring, and took careful aim.

Whp whistled the arrow, streaking in a shallow arc.

"Ha!" I cried, as the missile struck its target. I watched the squid flash red, vanish in a puff of smoke, turn into a small black organ-looking thing, and then sink right out of sight.

I won't tell you the word I shouted. I'm not proud of it, but I should win some kind of prize for making one syllable last a good five seconds.

"Frrph," snorted Moo from behind my back as if to say, "What were you thinking? How did you not have a recovery plan?"

"I don't know," I said, only now seeing solutions. "I should have tied something to the arrow, or found a way to make a net or . . . or even waited till a squid was closer to shore! But why didn't I think of it till now?"

I started pacing. "Idiot!" I grunted, wishing this world would let me hit myself. "Stupid, stupid idiot!"

"Moo!" interrupted my stern friend, forcing me to stop and face her.

"You're right," I said. "When looking for solutions, beating yourself up isn't one."

"Moo," replied the cow, as if to say, "That's better."

"I know I'm not an idiot," I said, calmly raising my hands, "but something *is* wrong with me, like my brain's only working part-time."

I started pacing again, more out of contemplation than anger. "It's not like panic or hunger. It's something new. Well, not new, actually. I've felt it coming on for a while, but now that I'm well-fed and not scared out of my wits, I can see this mental mud for what it is." I could feel anxiety rising, the last thing I needed right now.

"Any ideas?" I asked the animals. "Any hints about what's causing it?" Moo, along with Flint and Cloud, the white sheep, just looked at me.

"I don't have any either," I said, checking the setting sun, "and that's what really worries me."

Plodding back to my underground hideout, I tried to refocus my mind on fishing. I looked down at the pathetic little piece of spider silk in my pack. Just one try at the crafting table told me I couldn't tie it to an arrow. Likewise, I wasn't going to get a net out of a single strand. I'd need another length of spider silk, or . . .

I looked up from the crafting table, through my wall-sized window to the sheep grazing in the darkened meadow.

Wool!

"That's what those shears were for!" I shouted to them. "They're for collecting wool!"

Reenergized by this new theory, I began chanting the Way of the Five P's. Shears meant more iron, which meant more mining, which meant more torches and a pickaxe. Fighting through thickening thoughts, I still managed to plan, prepare, and prioritize clearly enough to get myself back down into the spiral staircase and looking for more iron.

I'm not sure how long it took. I was having trouble keeping track of time. When I found enough iron to smelt into a pair of shears and bring them out to my sheep peeps, it might have been a day and a half later.

"Don't worry," I said nervously, holding the U-shaped cutter next to Flint, "this won't hurt."

Please don't hurt, I prayed.

Snip went the shiny metal blades, slicing three blocks of black wool. "Yes, sir, yes, sir, three blocks full."

"Baa," responded my unhurt, but now very naked, friend.

"Don't worry," I reassured Flint, "it'll grow back."

Please grow back, I prayed, running the wool back to my observation room.

Had I been as sharp as the shears, crafting might have taken a few minutes. But my ever-dimming wits stretched the process into the early evening. Wool with spider silk, wool with sticks, wool with wool . . . by the time I'd moved on to wool with wood planks, the sun was long gone. That turned out to be a good thing actually, because placing the three wool blocks above three planks created the cure for my cloudy brain.

It was a bed. Nothing fancy, mind you, but still amazing to look at. The wood planks had transformed themselves into a four-legged frame. The black wool somehow became a white sheet, a red blanket, and a soft white pillow. Placing this new piece of furniture in the bunker, I did something I hadn't done since first waking up in this world. I yawned.

I need to rest, I thought. *Why didn't I think of this before? Because I need to rest. Duh.*

I still didn't feel physically tired, which was probably why I hadn't given sack time much thought. I'd also been so distracted with immediate needs like food and healing and not getting killed by monsters that I'd never considered my mind's need for slumber. Now, climbing into the little bed, resting my head on the pillow, and pulling the covers up to my neck, I gave another long-overdue yawn.

That's what those memories must have meant, was my last thought; cramped fingers, burning eyes, numb bum. They were memories of a sleepless night. But doing what? A job? Homework? A hobby? What had I been doing that kept me up so late?

"Tomorrow," I yawned, as the world faded to black. "I'll figure it all out tomorrow, 'cause nothing clears the mind like a good night's slee . . ."

CHAPTER 11

COURAGE IS A FULL-TIME JOB

I'd be lying if I said I remembered my dream, or even if I had any, but waking up the next morning confirmed what a good night's sleep could do for my mind. Imagine walking through fog, not so thick that you can't see your hand in front of your face, but just thick enough to blot out the landscape. That'd been me for so many sleepless days and nights. Now the fog had lifted and I could finally see where I was going.

Back to fishing, I thought, grabbing my shears. *Back to trying to make a net.*

"Hey Cloud," I said to the white sheep. "How'd you sleep? Do you sleep? Apparently I do, and it's really gotten the wheels turning. In fact" — I snipped off three fluffy cubes — "I was thinking that the only piece of the missing net puzzle is more wool."

Spying Flint a few paces away, I was relieved to see that his — or her? — beautiful black coat had grown back. "No problem if this doesn't work," I said, shearing off two more soft dark blocks and carrying them all to the forest-side crafting table, "because I just woke up with a backup plan."

Less than a minute and several wool-on-wool combinations later, I saw that the fishing net idea was out. "And that backup plan is," I told the sheep, "drumroll please . . . a fishing pole!"

"Baa," said Flint, who went back to eating grass.

"I know," I said. "Duh! The most obvious tool. What a difference a few Z's make."

Crafting a quartet of sticks, I placed them and the wool on the crafting table. While mixing and matching came up with nothing, my recharged brain was already on to a backup-backup plan.

"So wool doesn't work," I said, reaching for the length of spider silk in my pack. When that didn't work either, I moved on to the next logical step. And that's when my enthusiasm cooled.

"Maybe this world just won't let me make a fishing pole," I warily told the sheep, "and I'm kinda hoping that's true." An icy ball began growing in my stomach. "'Cause if it's not, then the only other option is getting another length of spider silk."

"Moo." The sound made me jump.

"Don't sneak up on me like that," I told Moo angrily.

"Moo," she retorted, telling me not to change the subject.

"It won't be that dangerous," I said, holding up my bow. "We know they're docile in daylight, so if I can pick one off at a safe distance . . ."

She snorted.

"I gotta try," I protested, holding up a handful of zombie flesh. "I can't keep living on this stuff."

"Moo," argued the cow, reminding me about the garden.

"Well, that's still a long way off," I said, "and we still don't know if I can eat it."

"Moo," questioned Moo, seeing that I wasn't telling her the whole story.

"No, I guess it's not just about food," I admitted, as thoughts and feelings rose from deep down in my gut. "It's about . . . courage."

Looking down at my shoes, I suddenly felt a twinge of shame. "I've been . . . afraid . . . of those mobs . . . always running from them, always thinking about what they can do to me."

"Baa," said Flint with a healthy dose of common sense.

"Yes, I know I should be afraid of them," I conceded. "If I wasn't I wouldn't be alive. I get that fear's a survival instinct, and I don't want to ever ignore it."

I looked down at the bow again, then up to my friends. "But I can't be a prisoner of it either. I need to know that if I have to fight I can, that I can control my fear instead of it always controlling me." I motioned to Disappointment Hill. "If I don't, I'll be cowering in a hole forever and that might be surviving, but it's not living."

Moo let out a low, resigned "moo." She knew I was making sense, even if that sense put me right in harm's way.

"Yeah, you're right," I answered, looking at the late morning sun. "I wish I had come to this conclusion last night. At least then I could have found a spider first thing this morning, instead of having to wait for one tomorrow."

Nothing is worse than waiting, counting the seconds, drenched in anxiety. Do you know the difference between anxiety and fear? I didn't until that day.

Fear is a real, present, right-in-your-face threat. Anxiety comes from a potential—or in this case, future—threat. Fear can be conquered. Anxiety has to be endured. And that's what I did. Walking around the island, talking to Moo or the other animals, going over in my mind how I'd kill the spider, all the while enduring wave after wave of mouth-drying, jaw-clenching anxiety.

At the crest of those moments, like waves on a stormy sea, were thoughts I'm still a little reluctant to talk about. They were thoughts of backing out. *The garden'll be ripe soon. Zombie flesh isn't so bad. There's no proof whatsoever that this world will let you make a fishing pole.* These are only some of the excuses I came up with to try to justify staying safe. As the day wore on, I could feel my nerve cracking, my will starting to give way. If this world had regular, twenty-four-hour days, I probably would have surrendered to cowardice.

As night fell I retreated to the bunker, got into my bed, and prepared for another recharging sleep. I didn't get it.

BANG BANG BANG BANG!

The clamor of zombie fists jolted me out of bed. A ghoul had come calling. "Get outta here!" I shouted, wishing this world would let me craft earplugs. "I gotta get some sleep."

"Guhhh," the zombie groaned, teasing my terrified heart.

"Yeah, well . . ." I won't tell you the last part of what I yelled. It wasn't my finest moment.

What I really should have said to the zombie was "thank you," because after a day of trying to make up reasons *not* to fight, I'd just been reminded of why I should.

Each punch of the putrefied fists helped batter my anxiety into resolve. "If I didn't have to save my only arrow," I growled at the grumbling ghoul, "you'd be a midnight snack."

By dawn, I was more than ready for battle. I watched the sun burn my would-be home invader into a smoldering chunk, which I washed down with a bucket of Moo's finest.

"No more waiting. Now or never." Bow in hand, I marched out the western door, and stopped short at the sight of a spider sitting just within the shade of the woods.

"Now or never," I whispered again, creeping slowly across the exposed, open field. The arachnid didn't notice me, or, true to my theory about daylight, didn't seem to care. It even turned away as I inched to within a dozen or so blocks.

Heart pounding, skin tingling, mouth dry as sand, I drew a short breath, and drew back my bow. The arrow rocketed skyward, thunking down into the spider's bulbous body.

And it did not die!

"Rsss!" rasped the eight-legged killer, eyes whipping around to lock squarely on mine.

"Oh . . ." I gulped.

I sprinted back for the safety of the hill. Hisses rang in my ears. Cold, jagged fangs ripped down my back. I fell forward, stumbling, gasping, running for my life as more bites tore at my exposed flesh.

No amount of adrenaline could push me past the slicing fangs. No amount of hyper-healing could counter their continuous blows. A third strike knocked me against the side of the hill. I kissed dirt, felt my front teeth crack, and saw that I'd never make it to the open door.

"Sssp!" hissed the exultant arachnid, crouching for its final leap.

"Enough!" I shouted, grabbing the stone axe from my belt. I spun, swung, and caught my attacker in midair. Crude stone slammed into crimson eyes, throwing the spider back and buying me enough time to run. Only I didn't run. I charged!

Snarling like a zombie, I struck the spider again. It hissed. I hit. It leaped. I chopped. A final rasp, a puff of smoke, and my first standup battle was over. And to the battered, tattered victor went a length of thin, white silk.

"Moo!" called my congratulatory friend, along with a few celebratory "baas."

"Thanks, but . . ." I huffed, grabbing the sticky twine. "I just hope it works." Slouching painfully over to a crafting table, I placed my sticks and string. I coughed as my hyper-healing tried, and failed, to rejuvenate me on an empty stomach. "Gotta work . . ."

And it did!

Three diagonal sticks and two vertical lengths of silk later, I was showing off my new invention to Moo.

"Look!" I cried, then collapsed into a hacking fit. "No . . . no more zombie flesh."

My creation looked pretty much as you'd expect: a long wooden rod with a short line at the end. The crafting table had even given me a hook and a little red and white mini-square bobber. At least I thought it was a bobber. It suddenly occurred to me that I had no memories of fishing. I must have seen the bobber in pictures or heard about it from someone else. That's probably why I hadn't considered another important fishing aid until now.

"Don't hooks need some kind of bait?" I asked Moo nervously. "Or a lure?"

"Moo," responded the even-tempered cow, reminding me that I didn't need to attract the squid to catch it.

"Right, sorry," I said as the flash of panic subsided. "I just need to cast out and snag it, which means I better practice snagging." Hobbling to the north shore, I whipped the hook out to sea.

"I'll say this for spider silk," I told Moo, "it sure does stretch." I was about to pull in my line for another practice cast when I noticed the water bubbling. To be more specific, I saw little mini-squares of water popping up on the surface all around my bobber. "Was it always this way?" I asked Moo. "Did I just not notice it before?"

Moo's response sounded like "What do you think?"

"Couldn't be," I answered. "It's gotta be because of the hook. But why?"

I couldn't see any squids around. I couldn't see anything except the water and that new—

"Trail!" I yipped as a V of bubbles appeared off to my far right.

"What is it?" I asked nervously, "What should I do?"

All the fear I'd faced with the giant spider suddenly came rushing back. Was that a squid far below the surface, or a bigger momma squid, or some giant sea monster I hadn't even seen before? Was it about to grab my hook, pull me in, drag me into its open, tooth-filled . . .

"Be brave!" called Moo, forcing me to stand my ground. "Think of all the fear you've conquered, all the anxiety you've endured, to get to this point! Don't throw it all away now!"

"You're right!" I hollered, amazed at how much wisdom she could cram into one simple moo. "Courage is a full-time job."

The water splashed, the bobber sank, and I felt a strong tug on my line. I yanked back hard, expecting to see some subsea behemoth exploding up at me. Instead, a little bluish gray creature, about the size of my hand, flew out of the water and into my belt.

"A fish!" I exclaimed. "There's fish in the sea!" I didn't worry about why I couldn't see them, or how this one had been attracted to my hook. Immediately I chomped into the soft, smooth skin, and was immensely relieved that my mouth and hand cooperated.

"Moo," called Moo, halting my chewing and reminding me of the dangers of raw food.

"Right," I told her. "Sushi's great, but we don't know if this is sushi-grade fish."

Limping back to my bunker, I was relieved to see that the furnace also complied, filling my room with an enticing, familiar smell. The flames turned the bluish fish to gray, and the flesh from a slippery slime to flaky white perfection.

"Delicious fish," I mumbled, savoring each mouthful as my hyper-healing roared back to life.

"More," I moaned, and stepped outside onto the eastern

beach. Just like before, I cast out my line and waited for the seas to boil. It took a little longer this time—who knew fishing required patience?—but after a minute or so, I saw another bubbling V. I waited for the bite, felt the tug, and yanked back hard. This time, a small pink-and-red fish with a pronounced lower jaw flopped into my hand.

"You look like a tasty salmon," I told my dinner. "Now let's see if you taste like one."

Turning back for the bunker, my eyes happened to fall on the wheat garden. There were three squares of ripe grain.

From famine to feast, I thought, plucking up the golden stalks and carrying them over to the beachside crafting table. Three seconds and three vertical stalks later, I was holding a soft, warm loaf of bread. And it tasted great! Light and tangy like a baguette straight from the oven.

That's all it took, I marveled, *just three stalks to "bake bread."*

"Moo," came a call from the hilltop above.

"Yes, that's true." I smiled up at Moo. "The irrigation ditch must have made the wheat grow a lot faster."

"Moo," she continued, this time with a chastising edge to her voice.

"If I'd checked on the garden earlier," I conceded, "I wouldn't have had to take such a great risk for a fishing pole. But then I never would have found my courage."

CHAPTER 12

RISK AND REWARD

"Good morning," I called out to my grazing friends. "Look what I just learned."

I held out yesterday's uncooked salmon.

"Notice anything different?" I asked. "Exactly! There is no difference! Because I just discovered that this world keeps everything preserved."

"Baa," said Flint, turning with Cloud for another patch of fresh grass.

"Yeah, maybe for you that's no big whoop," I said, "but in my world, food spoiling is a huge deal. Back in the day we had to dry or salt or . . . I think that's why spices were invented. I'm sure I heard that once. Even now, everything's gotta be frozen or refrigerated or packed with preservatives, which can be just as dangerous as spoiled food. But this"—I gave the salmon a reassuring sniff—"this means I don't have to waste any time trying to figure out how to store my grub. I can bank as much as I need for as long as I need it, which means I got hunger licked!"

"Frrph," snorted Moo, warning me not to celebrate just yet.

"Right," I agreed, grabbing my fishing pole from my pack. "The garden's still tiny and the fish won't catch themselves."

After crafting an outdoor furnace, and breakfasting on rich, oily salmon, I parked myself on the island's southern shore and spent the rest of the morning fishing. I can see why so many people in my world do it for fun. There's the anticipation of a first bite, the thrill of feeling something on your hook, and that last moment before you reel in your catch when you wonder exactly what's on the line.

That last part really came into play when I discovered how many different things swam in the sea. In addition to the salmon and the little blue-gray fish were two other species that I immediately recognized from home. The first was striped orange and white, and the second was yellow, roundish, and spiky. Like I said, I may not have personally fished back in my world, but I'd seen enough movies or gone to enough aquariums to know that these were "clowns" and "puffers." Since neither turned out to be cookable—and I wasn't going to risk poisoned sushi—I packed them away for some possible future use.

Ironically, my third inedible catch was the exact reason I'd started fishing. Squids are a real pain in the . . . well . . . the lower rear portion of my body that this world won't let me sit on. They don't come to your hook like fish, and when I did manage to snag one, it kept wriggling free. After several exasperating attempts, I got one close enough to the shallows to hack it to death with my axe. And then, as a final insult, I found out that the little bit of black meat it dropped wasn't really meat but a gland my mouth wanted no part of.

"Whatever," I said with a shrug to Moo, examining the three salmon and half dozen blue-gray fish in my pack. "Maybe just a few more, just to be safe."

Whipping the hook out to sea, I waited for the inevitable V. A few minutes later, I spotted one, and braced for the mild jerk of a bite. But it wasn't mild at all. It was harsh and powerful, as if something much bigger than a fish was at the other end of the line.

"Whoa!" I blurted, nearly dropping my pole. Was I right about a momma squid, or a giant sea monster? "Be brave." I gulped and yanked the quivering rod.

I never would have expected, never could have imagined, what popped up from the bubbling surface. Not a fish, not a monster, but a pair of old, raggedy leather boots. "Are these mine?" I asked Moo. "Do ya think they fell off my feet when I woke up in the sea? Could they have just drifted here with the current?"

If that wasn't the answer, then someone else must have made them . . . and at that moment, the world around me felt much bigger.

Putting them on, I found they fit snugly over my painted-on shoes. "They have to be mine," I said, "unless everyone in this world has the same shoe size." I took a few practice steps. "And they feel pretty good, too, and the extra padding really helps cushion my feet."

"Frrph!" scolded Moo, who began to walk away.

"Yes, I know they're cowhide," I argued, following her, "but I can't just throw them away. I mean, yeah, they're a little ratty and all, but the extra foot protection . . ."

The word stopped me in my tracks.

Protection.

A few days ago, I never would have made this mental leap, but now my well-fed, well-rested brain latched on to the concept of safety.

"Do you think," I asked Moo, striding over to where she was lunching with Cloud, "this world will let me make more clothes out of other materials?"

"Baa," said Cloud, now with a fully regrown coat.

"No, no, I don't mean wool," I told the sheep. "I mean iron. I mean armor."

"Moo," said the cow, voicing a ton of questions.

"Armor," I repeated. "Something I can wear over my clothes that will stop a zombie punch or a spider bite."

"Baa," asked Cloud.

"No, I'm not sure I can do it," I answered. "I don't know if this world will let me. But now that I've conquered hunger, the last basic need is safety."

I took off the boots, gesturing with them to the horizon. "And once I cross mob attacks off the list, I can stop worrying about survival and start asking the really big questions."

"Moo," said Moo.

"Yep," I answered, looking at the ground beneath my feet. "Looks like I've got a lotta mining to do."

Loading up on torches and a couple of spare pickaxes, I headed down the spiral staircase. It was slow, boring work, one gray block after another. I did have a few false alarms, though, when I started coming across other types of rocks. They were all speckled gray, white, and pink. They were also utterly useless, and not even worthy of a name.

It was almost a relief to break the monotony with a pocket of dirt. Using my shovel, I started scooping, and let out a resounding "aww yeah!" as the last cube revealed a wall of iron ore. "End of the line," I chirped, not realizing that it was just the beginning.

Behind the eight orange-flecked blocks, I discovered an entirely new ore. This one was red, and like coal and iron, embedded in standard gray rock. "Now, that's kinda cool," I said, as the first strike of my pickaxe caused the small cherry freckles to glow.

Now, if you know of any similar kind of substance in our world, feel free to add a footnote to this story for any future travelers. But since I've never seen or heard of anything close to this red stone, I'm just going to call it "redstone."

Later, much later, I'd learn that this was one of the most valuable, useful commodities of this world. At the time though, I was so ignorant that I didn't even know how to mine it. I tried a few swipes with my stone pickaxe, but all that did was obliterate the entire rock.

Maybe an iron pickaxe would do better, I thought, deciding to put iron tools ahead of iron clothes.

After climbing back up to the bunker, I threw the raw ore into the furnace, then carried the finished ingots out to my forest-side crafting table. After making an iron-tipped pickaxe, I tried my hand at anti-mob fashion.

Ninety seconds later, I had my answer.

"This world will let me make armor!" I called to Moo, holding up an iron cap.

Donning my new helmet, I was shocked at how light and comfortable it felt. Wasn't armor supposed to be the opposite: heavy and hot and really scratchy?

"How cool is this?" I asked, strutting around the grazing cow. "Comfy *and* monster proof."

"Moo," warned my ever wary friend.

I answered with a dismissive wave. "I won't assume anything until it's properly tested. On the other hand, I'm not gonna stop mining while I wait for that test to happen."

After another restful, dreamless sleep, I raced downstairs like it was Christmas morning, which it kinda was considering how many presents were waiting for me below. The thought of more iron, and this new mysterious redstone, was enough to lighten my every step.

I'll cut to the chase. The iron pickaxe let me mine the redstone out of the rock, but after some quick underground crafting experiments, I wasn't able to make anything more than a torch. And that dim, sputtering little torch, by the way, didn't throw nearly as much light as the regular coal-tipped model.

"Well, that's a letdown," I said, pocketing the rest of the redstone. I turned to my new shiny metal pickaxe and said, "but at least I got you now."

And what a leap over the stone model that was! Not only is an iron pickaxe twice as efficient, but it can take twice the punishment as well.

Now the Iron Age has come, I thought, knocking stone after stone aside. *Better tools and armor and . . . who knows what else I can make!*

Half a day later, I'd mined enough iron to craft a chest plate or breast plate or whatever the proper term is for an iron shirt. Just like the helmet, it was light as a feather, and just like the doors and hatches of this world, the arms moved on invisible joints. "Perfectly flexible," I called out to Moo, waving my stone axe in mock battle. "A few more hauls and I'll look like a hero from a fantasy novel, or from the real Dark Ages."

At that, Moo shot me a curious look.

"No, it wasn't actually dark," I explained, "more like an expression for dumbness. It was this place and time when people didn't read, and bathed, like, never, and fought a lot because they couldn't think of anything better to do. And because they fought so much, they had to wear iron clothes and . . ."

My voice trailed off. Now that I had the image of a floating, full suit of armor in my head, I saw the natural accompaniment that had escaped me until that moment.

"SWORD!" I shouted to Moo, the sheep, and anyone and anything that would listen. "I GOTTA MAKE A SWORD!"

I hit the stairs at light speed. "Please, world, let me make a sword," I prayed, picking through endless stones.

The gray wall fell away, revealing dim orange spots. I couldn't wait to get upstairs; I had to know right then. Sweating as my new furnace turned the little hollowed-out chamber into a sauna, I cursed this world for not letting me cross my fingers.

I didn't need to. It worked! Just one stick under two iron ingots gave me a weapon of lethal beauty.

"You are safety," I told the sword, "for you are strength."

And yes, if you're wondering, this world *will* let you make both a stone and wood sword if you want. And yes, I'm not exactly pleased with myself for not thinking of it sooner. But let's just remember the rule about not dwelling on past mistakes, shall we, and focus on the accomplishments of the present.

"You need to be named," I told the double-edged blade. "Isn't that what the little guy in that story did after he killed the giant spider, or when that king pulled his sword from the stone? That's kinda what I did, plus a few extra crafting steps. He had Excalibur, whatever that means, and I have . . ."

I kicked around a bunch of awesome names: Slayer, Storm-brewer, and Fire of the Eternal Flame. What I settled on didn't sound as cool, but better exemplified what this weapon meant to me.

"Since your job is to protect me," I said, "you will forever be known as Protector."

And with a few theatrical slices, I added, "And just wait till the nightscum up top taste your wrath."

"Squeak."

I froze, wondering if I'd just heard my own boots.

"Squeak."

No, not me. This was something else, something close, something that had to be right behind the rocks.

"We got company," I told Protector, and switching it for my iron pickaxe, tried to trace the source of the noise.

Remember how I said a while back that sounds on the island have the annoying habit of coming from all directions? Well, it's no different underground. The first tunnel I made must have been in the completely wrong direction, because a minute or so in, I heard the squeaking sounds fading. Turning around, I only tunneled a little way before the stone block in front of me suddenly vanished. And I don't mean cut out or disintegrated. I mean it literally poofed away like a dead mob!

In its place was a small, gray, prickly creature that looked like a crab and a porcupine had a child. "Well, hi there," I said, stepping up to what I thought was a perfectly harmless critter. "It's nice to meet—OW!" I jumped back as little teeth stabbed through the leather of my boot.

"Why, you little . . ." I began, but let out an undignified "yeee!" on the second bite.

"Get outta here!" I squealed, backing up the stairs. It wouldn't leave me alone, snapping and nipping and doing its best to tick me off.

"I'm warning you!" I said between yips and yelps. "Seriously! Don't make me have to—"

The next bite was its last, as one good sword swipe made for one dead "crabupine."

"Sorry you didn't have a more heroic debut," I told Protector. "But we now know the source of the noise."

And then, on cue, came another squeak.

"Or not," I said, realizing that the little toe biter had backup. Sword raised, I stepped cautiously back into the crabupine's tunnel. This time I didn't even need the pickaxe as two more stones puffed into a pair of gnashers. "Well," I said, slicing them into dust, "at least now I know to make some iron shoes for—"

"Squeak."

Seriously, I thought, wondering how many more annoying crabupines lay in wait.

"Squeak," came the sound, closer than ever.

"Wait a minute," I said, taking a moment to listen. The sound I'd been hearing all this time was close, but not exactly like a crabupine's crackling SNAP. This was more of a squeak like you'd hear from a mouse or a rat.

"Great," I said sarcastically, "now I get to have my toes nibbled by vermin."

Pickaxe in hand and sword in belt, I bashed away at the stone wall in front of me, and gasped when a block fell away into pitch black. Hot, moist air whooshed through the opening, along with a small, brown, winged creature.

Bat! I thought, and drew Protector. Didn't bats suck your blood? Would it go for my neck or my eyes? The answer was neither, as the birdlike rodent flew right past me and up the staircase to the surface.

"You better be the last thing I find down here!" I called after it, grateful that I didn't hear any more squeaks.

I cleared out the tunnel's second stone, making an entrance tall enough to walk through. Before taking one more step, however, I made sure to place a torch on the floor in front of me. Its flickering light barely touched the walls and ceiling of a truly massive cave.

I could see several collections of coal, redstone, and, to my great joy, iron, all embedded in the nearby walls. "Jackpot!" I shouted, rushing past the circle of light. More torches revealed more iron, more coal, more . . .

CLICK.

I froze.

CLICKETY-CLACK.

Bones? No, can't be. Not down here.

An arrow whistled out of the darkness, striking me in the shoulder. I spun, more from the impact than the actual wound, as the iron shirt had stopped it from going too far in. To my utter shock, I saw a skeleton archer clattering into the glow.

"How'd you get down here?" I asked, raising Protector. "Can you spawn underground as well!?"

My enemy answered with another arrow, this one hitting my ironclad chest. I winced, charging forward with Protector poised to strike. Two arrows, yes two, met me halfway. The first came from the skeleton in front of me, the second from the darkness behind it.

Wha . . . where . . .

Stunned but not deterred, I tried another frontal assault. A pair of projectiles knocked me back. Now I could see the second skeleton, clacking out of the shadows to plant a well-placed arrow in my chest.

"You're"—I paused as another volley punctured my shirt—"you're not even s'posed to be down here!"

Still reeling from surprise and disbelief, I hesitated just long enough for another twin shot to kick me back. Looking like a pin cushion, I now saw that my present strategy could only get me killed. Even at my quickest run, I'd never get close enough to hit them, and my armor and hyper-healing would only hold for so long. I'd never outlast the bombardment.

"All right then!" I shouted, turning and running for the exit. "You come to me!"

Zig-zagging through the endless barrage, I pranced back into the safety of the tunnel. The boneys were clicking just a few steps behind.

Good, I thought, hiding off to the side of the entrance.

Earlier I'd learned about the value of thinking under pressure. Now I had my first chance to practice it. Distance, I realized, was the ally of the bow and the enemy of the sword. Cramped quarters, however, might just even the odds.

As the first fleshless face clacked into view, I slammed my blade right into it. The skeleton pivoted toward me, shooting point-blank into my leg. I hissed as the arrow lanced deep into my unarmored thigh. "Now you die!"

A final slash and the sniper puffed away. Before the smoke cleared, the second thoughtless bonehead took its place. This time I learned enough to keep to the corner of the chamber, just close enough to strike, but obscured enough to prevent a clean shot.

"Eat this, Boneboy!" I growled, as my blade sent the second skeleton to meet his partner. I slumped against the rear stone wall and reached frantically into my belt for some fish. The one I'd brought along as a snack was enough to close most of my wounds and dissolve the forest of arrows growing out of my chest. As they vanished one by one, I saw that the holes they'd made in my armor remained.

"Gotta learn to fix those," I said, seeing that Protector had also taken a few scratches.

Looking down at my feet, I saw that the skeletons had left me several war trophies. I picked up another bow, two more arrows, and two dry, bleached leg bones. As I examined them in my left hand, the image of white powder appeared in my right.

Okay, now, if you already know what bone meal is for then give yourself a pat on the back. Oh, that's right, this world won't let you, just like it wouldn't let me pull an arrow out of mine. At that point, however, I couldn't care more about ground-up dead skeletons than the danger of more live ones underground.

"How do they do it?" I shouted, bursting through the door of my observation room. "How do mobs spawn in caves?"

"Moo," replied the munching cow, as if to say, "They just do."

"I thought it was safe down there," I complained, pacing angrily in front of her. "The whole point was to get stuff to protect me from the mobs up here!"

Moo snorted tersely.

I sighed. "I guess you're right. It's still totally worth it because whatever I find to protect me up here will also protect me down there." I took off my iron shirt, examining the cheese grater holes. "It's just hard to accept that there's gonna be challenges everywhere I go."

Moo snorted again.

"Good point. The sooner I accept it, the easier it'll be to prepare for it." I slid my battered armor back on, and pulled out my battle-tested sword. "Great risks come with great rewards."

CHAPTER 13

WHEN THE WORLD CHANGES . . .

"I have to change," I told Moo. "Now that I know mining includes monsters, I have to change the Planning and Preparing part of my Five P's."

"Moo," said the cow with what could be a sarcastic "ya think?"

"I need a new plan for fighting; maybe a lot of it down there," I continued, "which means preparing a lot more food for hyperhealing." I glanced around at the forest, imagining what it would look like after dark. "It also means getting back to my nighttime studies of the mobs just to make sure that I'm not missing any details about their behavior. Which also means"—my eyes fell to my sword—"experimenting with all the resources I have, just to make sure I'm not missing any other weapons."

Swapping my sword out for the skeleton bone in my belt, I said, "Who knows what I can get from this." What I ended up getting was a blast from my frustrating past. Even worse this time because I couldn't blame my failures on hunger or sleep deprivation.

"What's the point!?" I griped to Moo, holding up the worthless white pile. "If I can't eat it or burn it or make it into something useful, why would this world let me gather it?"

In a rage, I threw a pinch of it onto the ground, and jumped back in shock as the flat green surface beneath me suddenly blossomed into tall grass and flowers.

I looked down at the remaining two pinches.

"Baa," said Flint, finishing my thought.

"Plant food." I punched up the tall grass for their seeds. "That's what this stuff is used for!"

Who knew plants needed to eat?

"Cluckcluckcluck!" I turned to see that the two chickens had shown up. "Can I help you?" I asked with mock formality. "Splashing in the lagoon suddenly not as exciting as—"

"Cluckcluckcluck," they interrupted, their eyes focused on what was in my hand.

"The seeds?" I asked, suddenly remembering a similar encounter. Hadn't the other chickens, the one's that the creeper blew up, been staring at me the last time I'd had seeds in my hand? Hadn't I been wondering about that right before the explosion?

"This is what you want," I said, holding out my hand. "Isn't it?"

Two sharp pecks and two of the four seeds were gone. And if you've never seen this happen, trust me when I tell you that I did *not* make this next part up. Little red hearts, like the type you'd see in some old-timey cartoon, began rising from the two fowl. "You seeing this, too?" I asked Moo.

The lovestruck cluckers walked over to each other, stood eye to eye, then parted as a tiny white chick popped into existence between them.

"So *that's* where babies come from!" I exclaimed. "At least in this world."

I tried repeating the same process, but the parents ignored my offering. "Got it," I said, "You're full. And besides, I could use extra bread."

Running over to the garden, I planted the seeds in a new row opposite my irrigation trench. Then, reaching for the last two pinches of bone meal, I spread them out on a pair of nearly mature stalks. Instantly the target squares ripened. "This is getting better and better," I said, without realizing how much better that day was about to get.

Harvesting the wheat gave me four—that's right, four—

packets of new seeds. "Awesome!" I cried, replanting them then rushing back to tell my friends.

"Guys!" I called, waving the golden grain. "Sometimes you get extra seeds! I can expand the garden without having to find more."

"Moo!" cried Moo, strangely matching my enthusiasm. Completely out of character, she and the sheep began stampeding toward me.

"Whoa, what's the matter?" I asked, looking over their heads to make sure nothing was chasing them. At the same time, I switched out the wheat in my hand for my sword.

The animals stopped. The sheep even looked away. Then I got it.

"You want this," I said, holding up the wheat and recapturing their undivided attention. "Just like the chickens, you can also . . . uh . . . well . . . you know."

Feeling suddenly awkward, and wondering if my square cheeks were blushing, I held out the bushels to Flint and Cloud. Hearts flew, eyes met, and then the island had another resident.

"Happy Birthday!" I said to the adorable, rainy day–colored lamb. "Welcome to our tiny, crazy island, little Rainy." Turning to Moo, I was about to make some joke about having more mouths to feed. I stopped, however, when I saw her turn away.

Maybe she'd just lost interest, now that the wheat was gone. I hoped that was it. I hoped she wasn't thinking about the cow partner she'd lost, or the baby calf she'd never have.

"I'll bring you some more tomorrow," I told her, noticing the darkening sky. "Promise."

You're the only one of your kind, I thought sadly, walking back to the hill, *just like me. So if we're alone together, doesn't it mean we're not really alone?*

I shouldn't have tried to study the monsters that night. Remembering Moo's loss, as well as the first chickens, had dredged up all the buried trauma of the creeper attack. I should have gone right to bed, cleared my head, and started fresh the following night. But then again, reliving the attack was what led me to my next discovery.

It happened halfway through the night. I couldn't stop replaying the nightmare. I tried to focus on the mobs spawning right in front of me, on the real creepers gliding silently past my window. They all faded behind the flashbacks. I couldn't shake the roar of the blast, the pain of my wounds, the grisly images of meat and cowhide and . . .

Suddenly I was fully present, blinking the memories away. I ran down the tunnel to the bunker, over to the storage chest. There it was: the feather. I'd forgotten all about it, along with the chip of flint.

Don't beat up on yourself, I thought, taking them back to the observation room. *You found them at different times, and with so many different things to keep track of.* I placed them on the crafting table, with a single stick in between. *Now you're free to focus on fighting, and look at the deadly result.*

"Look!" I hollered to the window, holding up four new arrows. "Ya see these!?" Whether the mobs did or didn't, they'd sure feel them soon enough. "Now you'll get what you've been giving," I said to a nearby skeleton, "along with all the rest of you!"

To punctuate the point, a spider skittered past my window. "You'll never get as close," I told it, "as your brother did when I only had one arrow." I waved the multiple missiles at it. "And more important, I now know how to make them! And as long as I can get sticks from trees and flint from gravel and feathers from . . ."

I paused, lost in a new idea. *Seeds make more chickens,* I thought, *and the garden makes me extra seeds.*

"Moo!" called the approaching cow, apparently sensing my scheme.

"That's right," I replied. "Breeding free chickens for their feathers!" Moo just looked at me blankly. "What I mean by 'free,'" I clarified, "is that everything I make, like tools and weapons, takes a lot of effort and time and gathered resources like wood and stone and iron. But this chicken farming idea, all it takes are bonus garden seeds I would have gotten anyway. That's why they're free. Free feathers and"—I moved past the knot in my stomach at the revelation—"free food! I'm gonna need a heck of a lot of extra food if I'm gonna be fighting my way through that cave. And besides," I said, my mouth now watering involuntarily, "roasted chicken tastes good!"

"Frrph," snorted Moo, dampening my euphoric mood.

"No, it's not the same as eating you," I replied defensively, "or them." I motioned at the sheep family behind her. "I know you guys. We're friends. But those birds, they're just . . . just . . . I can't even tell them apart. Can you?"

Moo tried the silent treatment.

"I need this!" I pressed, refusing to be cowed by a cow. "I need all the help I can get if I'm gonna get enough iron and coal." Arguing with Moo had brought up an idea from the lower recesses of my mind. It was a theory I'd been mulling over for some time, and now felt confident enough to express.

"See that," I asked, pointing to the torch tree. "Since lighting it up, not one monster, not *one*, has spawned anywhere near it, which means that mobs can't spawn in torchlight, which means that if I can get enough coal to make enough torches to light the entire island, my quest for security is done."

I took a lump of coal from my belt. "Which means that I'm gonna need tons of this stuff, which means a lot of mining in that monster-infested cave." I waved the lump at the distant chickens. "Which means I need tons of free feathers and food."

"Moo," condemned the superior mammal.

"How can you judge me," I quipped, turning back for the bunker, "when all you live on is free food!"

"Moo," she tried to answer as I slammed the tunnel door.

"Debbie Downer," I grumbled as I got into bed, trying to shove any second thoughts into the back of my mind. "Well, you're not gonna dampen my mining morning."

And she didn't, or the entire week that followed. Yep, I said week. Up till now, I've been giving you the play-by-play, day-by-day. Now we can pull back because something awesomely awesome happened: a routine!

For the first time since waking up in this unpredictable world, I had seven manageable, controllable, reasonably predictable days. I got up every morning, slapped on my armor, grabbed my tools and weapons, packed up some bread and fish, and sauntered jauntily underground.

Every day filled my pack with more mineral wealth: coal, iron, and even that arcane redstone. While the last substance still confounded me, the first two kept my furnace humming. I learned how to make both iron boots and pants to match. By the second day I looked like a proper, if battle-scarred, warrior, and by the fourth day I learned how to repair my battle scars.

Ever heard of an anvil? Just like the hearts, I'd only seen them in cartoons—you know, like when one was dropped on a character's head. Now, after learning how to combine ingots into iron cubes, and after combining a line of cubes with an upside-down T of ingots, I got a thick, heavy, ridiculously useful appliance. Imagine the two slots of a furnace, side-by-side instead of up and down. You place the item you want fixed in the left slot, some extra iron in the right one and bam, good as new.

I fixed my armor, my tools, even my worn-out bow by combining it with the other worn-out bow I'd gotten from a vanquished skeleton. And that bow would come in real handy, because all that iron and coal didn't come cheap.

The first mob I killed outright was a zombie, and it wasn't at a safe distance. Day one, I was picking away at a deposit of raw ore when I heard that all-too-familiar growl. "You ready?" I asked Protector. "'Cause I sure am!"

As the green gurgler slouched into the torchlight, I stood ready with a sharp iron welcome. "Know what your problem is?" I asked, as Protector's first slash knocked the growler back on its rotting heels. "You're just too dumb to be afraid." Four slices, that's all it took. Four slices and the zombie was meat at my feet.

"And we're just getting started," I boasted to Protector.

I collected a lot of reeking flesh that week, as well as spider silk and skeleton bones. The last trophy fertilized the garden, which got more seeds, which . . . well, you get it.

Making more and more chickens, and having to chase them all over the island, brought home the need to corral them. Does the term chicken coop mean a fenced-in area, or an actual chicken house? For me, it was the former. I learned how to craft sections of wood fencing and placed them in a square in the meadow. Once I'd lured the birds in with seeds, I closed them up securely with double wooden gates.

I wasn't collecting any feathers yet. I figured I'd wait until I had more chickens than I knew what to do with. That's why I saved the few arrows I had for the only enemy I wouldn't touch with a half-mile pole.

The first time I saw a creeper was on my fifth morning in the cave. I came out of the small entrance tunnel, walked past the ever-expanding border of torchlight, and thought I spied something moving in the gloom. It must have seen me first because the armless, soundless bomb was already sweeping forward.

Fighting jitters, I backed up a few paces, drew my bow, and took aim. The arrow hit the creeper just as it was starting to sizzle. Flying back a few steps, it tried another charge. "I know how you feel," I said, loosing my next and final shaft.

As the smoke cleared, I saw something hovering in the creeper's place. It was a pile of little gray granules, and it didn't take a chemistry lab to deduce what they were.

Fire, tools, and iron—all my discoveries had mirrored the progress of my species. What else could be next but the mighty power of guns?

"This changes everything!"

It didn't. At least, not at that point.

Believe me when I say that I tried every experiment I could think of. I even tried setting the stuff on fire with a torch, which was not my brightest moment, to say the least. Fortunately for you, the reader, and especially for me, the moron, this world wouldn't let me blow myself up.

"Maybe it's part of a bigger process," I told Moo, collecting the hovering pile. "Maybe I need to make the gun first."

Setting the gunpowder aside, I tried combining wood and metal in every conceivable way. All I got was a rehash of everything I'd already built, and an exasperating reminder to be grateful for what you have.

Not like I really need it, I thought, finally calling it a night. *I got plenty of armor and weapons and I'm getting pretty darn good with both.*

So why didn't I stop, you ask? Why didn't I just gather up all the coal I'd mined to light the island to keep the monsters from spawning? The answer is I needed the coal to fuel the furnace to smelt the iron for all my armor, weapons, tools, and anvil to repair everything. But, you might say, I wouldn't need to smelt all that iron if I'd just saved the coal to light the island.

Well, for starters, there was the carrot.

Yes, carrot. For a while zombies had been dropping more than just their flesh. Sometimes one would leave me an ingot of iron, or a worn tool, but one time, I think around the end of the sixth day, my latest kill dropped a small, pointed, green-topped root I recognized instantly.

"Ahhhh," I said, picking it up. "What's up, Doc?"

What was up was a new source of food. Replanting it in the garden and sprinkling it with a little bone meal allowed me to soon have a whole new row of crops, which meant I could divert even more wheat seeds to chicken farming.

And then there was the bluestone—at least, that's what I'm calling it. It's this blue stone—hence the name—you get from rocks like coal or redstone, and as with the latter, I couldn't find a use for it. But the idea that there were even more minerals down there made me wonder what else might be waiting to be discovered.

So yes, there were practical reasons for going on, and that should be enough for anybody. But the real reason, the one I wouldn't even admit to myself back then, was that for the first time since landing in this crazy, scary world, I finally felt in control!

I knew what I was doing and I knew how to do it. Racking up win after win made me feel strong and powerful. You have to know what that feels like, especially after feeling so weak and powerless. Would you give all that up?

I might have never stopped if the world hadn't chosen to stop it for me.

I knew something was wrong the moment I opened my eyes and noticed that my left hand felt tingly. Had I slept on it wrong? No, that couldn't be the case. This world doesn't let me sleep on my side. Or does it? Could I roll over after falling asleep?

I tried shaking out my hand, walking around the room, dressing in iron, having breakfast, doing all the things I normally did, but the tingling wouldn't leave.

It wasn't a painful feeling like the kind of needles I had in the other world when my hand had gone to sleep. This felt slightly more sensitive, more alive. I didn't like the new feeling, though, for no other reason than that it was new.

I liked normal. Finally, normal was on my side. When everything was going my way, the last thing I needed was change.

I went down into the mines, just like I usually did, got out my pick, and started searching for another cache of minerals.

Mining went smoothly, and for a while I forgot about my left hand troubles. And then I heard the zombie moan.

"First of the day," I told Protector, as the ghoul slouched into the light. "Let's get this over with." I raised my blade to strike. And that's when I knew Mr. Normal had checked out. No more easy, four-strike kills. This meatbag took at least twice the punishment before going down, and not before giving me a few really painful punches in return.

I reeled back in surprise, shaking as the zombie turned to smoke. "Maybe it's just a one-off?" I asked Protector nervously. "Some kinda rare super-zombie?"

"Think again," answered the world, in the form of an arrow whistling past my face. I pivoted to see the arrow's owner, and since there was only one skeleton, I decided on a conventional charge. I took a few hits, winced at the healing wounds, and soon found that this new bonehead was just as durable as the zombie.

"What's happening!?" I blurted out, as my seventh or eighth strike finally turned my attacker to fertilizer.

Like a long-lost friend, panic arrived and drove my feet back onto the ground. "Something's up. The mobs are harder to kill. Everything's changed!"

Moo just looked at me calmly, and uttered her signature answer.

"Well, at least you're the same," I said, feeling a little relieved. Moo might not have been the most stimulating of conversationalists, but her steady, even demeanor was a tonic for my nerves.

"Okay," I breathed, "maybe I'm exaggerating just a little bit. But"—I looked down at my hand—"some things are definitely different."

Moo gave me a casual glance and ambled away. I followed her, talking all the while. "Do you think that can happen? That this world can literally change overnight?"

I looked around us, checking to see that everything else was the same. "If that's true," I began, starting to absorb more of Moo's serenity, "then what am I supposed to do about it?"

"Moo," she said matter-of-factly.

"What do you mean, 'change with it'?" I shot back. "What kind of lame blow-off statement is that?"

"Moo," she repeated, glancing in the general direction of my left hand.

I held up the tingling appendage, considering the weight of Moo's words. "Change with it," I said softly, then mused, "If this world's just made the monsters tougher to fight, maybe it's given me new ways to fight them!"

Gun! It was a pipe dream, I know, but hopefully one where the pipe was a gun barrel. "Thanks," I said, darting back to the hill. "You always know what to say!"

Once again I threw out all the previous day's wood-and-metal combos. Once again, I didn't get a gun. I did get something else, however; something that just the day before had been a losing combination.

"Shield!" I breathed, holding up the long, broad board. "Today I can make a shield!" And if that new invention didn't kill my fear of change, what happened next buried it for good.

Up until this point, my right hand had been for tools and weapons, while the left was for crafting. It had only opened to show me what I could make with materials. But now, did this new tingling sensation mean . . . ?

I reached for the ghostly image of the shield, and gasped as my left hand suddenly opened.

"YES!" I crowed, dancing out to show my pals. "I made a shield, the mob's fate is sealed, my protection is realed, all thanks to my shield."

"Baa, moo, baa," replied my chorus of talent judges.

"Okay, so maybe I didn't write songs in my former life," I said with a chuckle, "but at least I got extra protection now, along with Moo's super-important new lesson."

"Baa," said little Rainy, now a full-size sheep. They grow up so fast.

"Glad you asked," I answered, and motioning to Moo, announced, "When the world changes, you've got to change with it."

CHAPTER 14

ALWAYS BE AWARE
OF YOUR SURROUNDINGS

Yeah, I was happy for the shield, but dude, did it take some practice!

First off, it's big and bulky and it blocked my vision. I couldn't just carry it all the time if I didn't want to trip over something. Second, once I raised it for cover, I couldn't go any faster than a crawl. So that meant escaping was out. And third, raising it for cover meant I couldn't use my sword at the same time. I had to switch between attack and defense, which was a whole new, much more demanding, style of fighting. No more blind bashing. Now I had to think about each blow and calculate the timing of attacks. I guess that's what real armored warriors must have done back in my world. Like me, they probably complained at first, but like me, they also probably stopped complaining after their first battle.

That battle came after my day of training aboveground. Venturing back underground, I came out into the cave and right into the targeting gaze of a skeleton. It raised its bow. I raised my shield.

BONK!

My hand vibrated with the impact of the deflected arrow. *Just a fluke?* I wondered, looking up to see the bonehead reloading. *Poor aim and a lucky—*

BONK!

Another shaft glanced harmlessly off.

"No fluke," I said, as a third arrow fell to my feet. "No lucky angle or lousy aim on your part."

Grinning from ear to flat, barely visible ear, I strode slowly toward my foe. "This shield actually works! It totally, absolutely, legitimately . . ." I stopped pontificating the moment I peeked back up over the top.

The skeleton, still shooting, not only began to retreat, but did so in a side-to-side, kind of frenzied oval. "Are you afraid?"

Unable to answer, unable to do anything more than fire fecklessly against my mobile wall, the bag of bones clacked crazily around. I blocked another shot, waited for it to reload, then swung down hard with Protector. The skeleton reeled, then took another shot. Again I blocked, and again I struck. Back and forth to its inevitable end.

"A hearty thank-you," I told the new leg bone, "from my carrots and wheat."

"Uhhh . . ." came a howling moan, ending my witty, one-sided banter. Looking up, I spied an approaching zombie. Raising my shield, I absorbed the first blow without injury. *Just like the skeleton*, I told myself, and lowered the shield to strike.

Pow!

The punch took me right in the jaw.

"You're s'posed to pause," I barked angrily, and raised my shield again. After taking the next blow, I tried another slash.

"Oof!" I breathed through dented armor and bruised ribs.

"Guhhh . . ." groaned the ghoul, assailing my battered board. Retreating under a torrent of blows, I realized that shields didn't work in close combat. Whereas the skeleton had been a well-timed dance, this was more of a boxing match. "Just like we used to," I said, backing up a few paces.

Sliding the shield into my backpack, I shouted, "Time to change back!" and gave my attacker a good slash across the face.

With renewed speed and agility, I tried to keep just a few paces away. "You're tougher," I admitted, "which means I gotta be smarter." Step in, strike, knock it back, then retreat and wait for it to advance.

"Adaptation," I crowed, giving the ghoul another slash. "Isn't that what some wise old guy once said? Something about the key to survival not being strength but the ability to change?"

In a fitting response, the lumbering bruiser kept doing the only thing he and his kind had ever done: make a slow plodding path right for me. "That's why my ancestors conquered my world," I preached as Protector knocked him back, "and that's why the sabertooth cats and the giant bears and all the other stronger, tougher killers ended up in museums."

"Gruhhh," snarled the zombie, recoiling with another chop.

"And that's where you'll all be," I boasted, raising Protector for the coup-de-grâce, "when I finally conquer this—"

"Gahhh," gasped the ghoul, as my next blow knocked it out of sight.

"Uh?" I asked, sounding just like the creature I'd slain and taking a step forward to investigate. The zombie didn't disappear; there was no puff of smoke. This time it'd actually fallen out of sight, downward, and had nearly taken me with it.

"Whoooa!" I warbled, stopping short at the edge of a cliff. I hadn't been paying attention to where I was going. I'd been too focused on the fight.

The zombie battle had taken me farther and farther down the cave, past my torches and around a narrow bend. I didn't notice that the temperature and humidity had risen, or that there'd been a light up ahead. Only when I'd knocked the zombie over the edge of the cliff did I finally stop and stare.

Before me lay an underground canyon: deeper, wider, and

just, well, grander than my tiny island up above. For a moment, all I could do was stare in awe at this subterranean world. Now I saw the source of the growing heat. Streams of red-hot lava poured from several openings in the cliffs. These long bright columns fell into a vast, boiling lake. I could also see water, thin blue lines falling from walls and the ceiling, crashing down into the lava, turning the air into a stifling steam bath. Just looking at the spectacle below made me dizzy, and imagining one misstep was enough to pull me way back.

Venturing a few careful peeks, I thought I could see some dry land at the edge of the lava and water. How could I not investigate? Nothing wrong with curiosity, right?

Of course not, I reasoned, *as long as it's* careful *curiosity.*

I started to dig a descending tunnel just behind the cliff wall. Every few steps I opened a window to get my bearings. I broke out onto uneven but safe ground and stared up in amazement. The canyon made the first cave I'd discovered, which had once looked so monstrous, seem like a rabbit hole.

The heat down here was merciless, tropical. I could actually feel my lungs baking with each breath. I could also feel the sweat collecting under my armor, running down my back into my boots. And yet, as I took a few sloshing steps across this stifling sauna, I didn't feel the least bit of thirst. *Well, at least this world won't let me get dehydrated,* I thought, blinking away stinging drops, *and I don't seem to smell when I sweat, which is pretty cool.*

Cool . . . If only there was a way to beat the heat down here.

I noticed that the nearest waterfall ended barely a few paces from my feet. Maybe dipping said feet for a few minutes could . . .

"Bad idea!" I yelped as the current tried to wash me into the lava. Half running, half hopping, I got close enough to the fall's tipping point to contain it with a ring of cobblestone.

As the blue surge subsided, I gawked at the material it revealed. These were smooth black stones that I'm creatively calling "blackstone." I think by this point, we've established that I wasn't a geologist back home. Whatever their real name was, these rocks were beautiful to look at, and just for the sake of a souvenir, I tried to mine up a block. And trying was as far as I got, because my pickaxe's iron blade was about as effective as my bare hands had been against standard stone.

"Well, you ain't goin' nowhere." I shrugged at the shiny black surface, then froze when it answered with a "Guhhh."

I snapped to attention, sword and shield at the ready. Of course the blackstone hadn't groaned back at me. Something else, something stinky and very familiar, was somewhere down here with me.

I spun in a full circle. All was clear. Nothing by the light of the lava lake. "Guhhh," echoed another groan. Was Mr. Deadhead behind a rock wall? Or . . .

I crept over to the edge of the lava lake, trying to see if I could find him on the other side. Big mistake. Peering across the roiling soup, I heard an omnidirectional "oomph."

I thought I was being careful. At two blocks away, it's not like I was actually at the edge. No chance of accidentally falling in, right?

"Grahhh," came a snarling growl, then . . .

BANG!

Festering fists bashed me in the back, throwing me forward and toppling me into the lava.

All I could see was red, breathing it in, choking on liquid fire. It is an indescribable nightmare, the feeling of burning alive. First came the shock of adrenaline, then the worst pain I'd ever felt. I'd been beaten, I'd been bitten, I'd even been partially blown up, and yet, all that suffering could not hold a burning candle to boiling in molten rock. Imagine every cell across your body, every nerve ending, every sensor capable of feeling suddenly rising in one wailing chorus of hell.

And yet, it was the total immersion—the complete, body-wide attack on my system—that ended up saving my life. As the pain receptors under my skin literally burned away, I was left with one numb nanosecond to move. And move I did!

As the flames licked up before my blinded, sizzling eyes, I swam with all my might for the blackstone bank. I don't know when I climbed out of the scalding stew, or if I continued to burn on land. Whatever was left of my rational mind locked on to the memory of the waterfall. Stumbling . . . fumbling . . .

Mercy! I was bathed in soothing, quenching salvation.

BANG!

Rotting fists stabbed right through the water, knocking me back toward the flames. I swung wildly, eyes just beginning to hyper-heal. They caught a flash of rotting green. Protector swung, the impact of flesh and bone vibrating up through the blade.

Sight and mind cleared in time for me to see the reeling zombie and to realize that, by sheer luck, its back, not mine, faced the roiling lake. On instinct, I charged, smashing my shield into its body.

"Gugh," growled the ghoul as I dug in my heels, ground slowly forward, and pushed it into the incinerating sea.

If only I could have celebrated, or just watched it burn, or done anything, *anything* in the world except teeter backward as regenerating pain receptors swamped my brain. Grunts. Screams. Howls. I threw myself back into the waterfall for the briefest shred of relief. All I got was the sense memory of drowning.

Eat!

Wolfing down fish and bread, I could feel my body reform. And just as my physical nerves were putting themselves back together, my mental nerves fell apart.

Never again! I swore, fleeing for the safety of the tunnel. *Never go underground for any reason again!*

Stripped of my courage, traumatized to the core, I made it halfway up the stairs before another "Guhhh" stopped me cold.

They're waiting for me! I thought, sword shaking like grass in the wind. *They're everywhere!*

And then the voice came, not from my ears but from my head.

"Moo."

That calming, doofy call floated in through my memories. Somewhere above me was a pal who'd stuck with me through all my trials and triumphs. What would she, and my sheep friends, have to say about surrendering to fear?

Courage is a full-time job.

Nerves returning, sword straightening, I ascended the rest of the stairs. And saw, for the first time, that the cliff walls around me were practically riddled with tunnels. I'd been so preoccupied with the size of the canyon, so entranced with the awesome spectacle of lava, that I never noticed these mundane but nearly fatal openings. In fact, the zombie I'd just heard was growling at me from another cave opening across from mine.

"So that's where your friend came from," I said. Looking down, I could see another hole, just above the waterfall and just big enough for one of those reekers to slouch through.

"That's what that 'oof' sound was," I continued to the other ghoul, "him hitting the ground just before he pushed me in."

"Uhhh," moaned the monster as I shook my head with shame.

"At least I've learned something," I said with a sigh, "and now it's burned into my brain, so to speak. Always, *always* be aware of your surroundings."

CHAPTER 15

TAKE CARE OF YOUR ENVIRONMENT SO IT CAN TAKE CARE OF YOU

Standing on the edge of the cliff, feeling my courage and confidence return, I called out, "Not leaving yet, ya hear me? I'm just getting started down here!"

"Uhhh," moaned the zombie, prompting me to wave.

"C'mon over," I taunted, hoping to entice it into a death fall. "Come and get me."

I tried some more waving, some more coaxing, I think I even tried dancing, anything to trick it into taking one more step over the side. The ghoul just groaned a couple more times, then disappeared into the dark recess of its tunnel.

"Of course," I said with a sarcastic shrug, "the one time one of you mobile meatloafs does something smart."

With the mindset of a vigilant hunter instead of an awestruck tourist, I made a mental note of every cave and shadow and possible enemy hiding place. I also noted every mineral deposit, every seam of coal and iron and . . .

Is that iron?

I squinted at the bottom of the canyon, right next to the lava lake, at a collection of metal-flecked rocks. They had to be iron—what else could they be?—but their color seemed just a shade lighter than the orange ore I was used to.

Situational awareness, I told myself, venturing back down the stairs. *That's the official term, isn't it? Be aware of my surroundings.* Reopening the entrance to the canyon floor, my eyes flicked frantically in all directions. Likewise my ears scanned for any sound beyond the bubbling of the lake.

I stepped gingerly across the blackstone, shivering at the heat radiating up through my feet. One false step, one missed mob . . .

Stopping well away from the edge, I strategized how best to get to the other side. Option one meant tunneling around, which meant possibly breaking through into more lava. Option two meant placing cobblestone along the side to create a walkway, which meant possibly falling or once again, being pushed in.

Do I risk it? Is it worth it?

If I hadn't been so busy shuddering at either of these scenarios, if I hadn't been so traumatized by nearly being killed ten minutes ago, I probably would have come to option three a lot sooner. Standing on the blackstone, with water behind me and lava in front, I realized the solution.

"Water cools lava!" I cried, eyes darting from one to the other. "Just throw water on it!" I turned and started back for the tunnel entrance, then stopped with a shake of my head. "Why go back when I've got everything I need right here?"

Placing a new crafting table on the blackstone, I started to make a furnace, then jumped back as the crafting table promptly burst into flames. "Okay," I said, as the table puffed into smoke. "Blackstone transmits heat. Thanks for that tidbit, world."

Laying down a new layer of cobblestone—which, by the way, was a lot easier on my slowly baking feet—I soon had my ingots smelting.

I then built a cobblestone staircase right up to the base of the waterfall and filled my new bucket, then poured the liquid on the farthest blackstone block.

It worked exactly as planned. The canyon around me darkened as lava cooled to shiny solidified midnight. *Well,* I reassured myself, *at least something good came from washing away my garden that time.*

Scooping up the water, I repeated the process two more times, then walked out onto a warm but solid surface. "Let's see," I began, trotting over to the new, mysterious ore. "What are you?"

Placing a torch on the wall, I gasped. "GOLD!"

The word glittered as brightly as the bounty before my eyes. Back in my world, it was the purest symbol of wealth. People wore it, hoarded it, killed for it. A plethora of terms were as embedded in our language as the rocks before my eyes: *gold rush, gold standard, golden opportunity,* and now in my case, *gold fever.*

"Mine," I breathed hypnotically, the word taking on a double meaning. "Mine!"

Attacking the rocks like an enemy in battle, I picked furiously for the irresistible ore. Two, three, four, five . . .

As the sixth gold-flecked stone fell away, I gaped at what lay behind it. These freckles were lighter, whitish blue, and sparkled like the stars.

"Oh my," I whispered as a few swings freed the lustrous, finely cut gems. "DIAMONDS!"

Minutes later I was rushing up to the surface, bars of gold in one hand and a collection of diamonds in the other.

"I'm rich!" I trumpeted, dancing my victory dance across the meadow.

The animals just looked at me for a minute, then went back to gobbling green.

"Don't you understand?" I asked, waving the wealth at them. "Don't you know what this means?"

Moo snorted with a sidelong glance.

"Yes, well." I tried to blow past her response. "I know I can't buy anything with it on this island but just look at it! Look how beautiful, how . . . useful!" Running over to the crafting table I shouted, "I mean, if iron is stronger than stone, then . . ."

I held up the glinting golden helmet. "See!"

"Moo," countered the cow, forcing me to compare the two headpieces. True, the golden model looked prettier, but the metal itself seemed flimsier, softer, and less likely to protect me than iron.

"Yeah, well, probably won't make *that* much of a difference," I argued, refusing to admit she was right. Going back to the crafting table, I placed the two diamonds I'd gathered above a single stick, and came away with the hardest, sharpest, most dazzling sword you can imagine.

"Ha!" I belted. "Whaddaya say to this?"

Moo didn't say anything, and neither did the two parent sheep. At least I got an agreeable "baa" from Rainy.

"Told ya this stuff was valuable," I strutted, marveling at the flashing blade. "Move over Protector," I said, packing away the obsolete iron cutlass, "because it's time for Flash."

Swaggering back to the hill, I called over my shoulder, "Who knows what else I can make with more diamonds and gold!"

Weapons, armor, maybe even new devices I hadn't thought of yet. These were all justifications for the desire driving my feet. I'd fallen victim to a lot of things on this island: hunger, fear, sleep deprivation, and now greed.

"We're in the money," I sang, recalling a tune much older than me. "La da dee dee dee . . ."

Stepping down into the cave, I might have continued to saunter carelessly into the gloom, but thought I saw a figure up ahead. Not a zombie or a skeleton. It was dressed head-to-toe in black with a tall hat, and, to my great excitement, had healthy, normal skin. It was a person!

"Hey!" I shouted, sheathing my sword and running forward. "I'm not alone anymore! I've got company!"

Getting close enough to touch, I babbled, "Where'd you come from? How did you get here? What's your—"

Glass shattered across my armor, the shards of a bottle thrown by my new "friend."

Suddenly my body slowed, my limbs feeling like lead. "Whaahaaveyouuudu . . ." I slurred as a second bottle broke across my face.

Nausea.

Pain.

Poison!

Blood burning, lungs squeezing, I fumbled clumsily for my weapons.

"Hahahaha," cackled my foe, actually taking pleasure in my suffering. This wasn't a dumb beast acting on pure instinct. This being could think, could feel, could choose to do me harm. This was what my world judged as evil.

"W-w-witch," I mumbled as another bottle appeared in its hand.

My diamond blade flashed. The witch tottered back. Fighting through waves of dizziness, I cut the laughter into smoke.

Food!

But my pack was empty. In my mad rush for riches, I'd totally forgotten to restock. Something was hovering at the witch's final resting place. Sugar?

Snatching up the little white pile, I staggered up to the surface.

SNAP!

A second battle, the one within my body.

SNAP!

Poison versus hyper-healing.

SNAP!

Would I make it? Could I reach the surface in time?

Crashing through invisible walls of agony, I stumbled back up into my bunker and over to the storage chest.

Fish!

The last two salmon went down just as the poison ebbed. "Ugh," I groaned, slumping forward, cooling my face on the smooth rock wall. It took several moments for me to feel well enough to move again. And when my body did, my mind still had a long way to go. *Are witches the only people in this world?*

"You'll never guess," I said, shuffling out into the clean, crisp air of the meadow, "what was down there."

"Moo," replied my friend sympathetically.

"Thanks for not judging me on this one," I said, twitching with the recent memory of pain.

Reaching into my pack for the bucket, I added, "And thanks for all the milk as well." Topping off the pail, I crafted and filled two more. "I hope this works as well on poison as it did on zombie flesh."

"Moo," said my generous pal, no doubt seeing the troubled look on my face.

"No, you're right," I agreed, "this wasn't just another battle with a new kind of mob. This was different." I paused to sift my feelings into words. "This was so disheartening because, well . . . after all this time I finally found someone like me."

"Moo," corrected the caring animal, with a distinction that made all the difference.

"Right again," I said with a nod, "it wasn't like me, it just *looked* like me and just 'cause someone looks like you doesn't automatically make them a friend."

GRRRP, growled my stomach, responding to the smell of the milk. "Gotta finish healing," I said, and went inside for my fishing pole.

Stepping out the back door, I noticed that three squares of wheat were ripe. *One loaf should be enough to restore me*, I thought.

I was about to combine the three bushels when I noticed something I'd never had before. Remember way back when I'd tried to combine all my edible ingredients like wheat and sugar and milk into something but for some reason it never seemed to work? And remember when I realized that the key to combining wheat was just more wheat? Well, now I not only had more wheat, but two lumps of sugar, three buckets of milk, and a baker's dozen eggs.

"Maybe now?" I said aloud, arranging them all on the crafting table. Four seconds later: "Piece of cake!"

No, literally! Hovering in the ether was a light brown, frosted confection complete with little red sprinkles.

"I knew there had to be an answer," I told Moo, setting the large, round, yummy cylinder on the ground. Yes, the ground. For some reason you can eat a whole loaf of bread but cake's gotta be eaten in slices. Go figure.

I took one bite, and let out a long, low zombie-like "mmm."

Now, if you like desserts, and if you don't there's something seriously wrong with you, then imagine going without them for nearly a month. Imagine living on a diet of fish, bread, and carrots, none of which had any spices in them by the way, and suddenly biting into a slice of heaven!

"Oh," I groaned again, savoring the spongy, moist cake.

"You know," I said to Moo, "this is the first sweet thing I've tasted since the . . ."

The word stuck in my mouth for a moment. "Apples."

Suddenly the cake didn't taste so good. No amount of sugar could counter such bitter memories.

"They were so delicious," I confessed sadly. "So crunchy and sweet and I burned up the trees that could have made more." My mind flashed to the accidental replanting of birch saplings and how easily they could have been oaks.

"I'll never taste an apple again," I said, shaking my head. "They're all gone forever because I thought the saplings were worthless."

I took off my gold hat and looked at it. "Worth," I repeated to Moo. "I think the word means how much you want something and how hard it is to get. I sure understand that meaning now, because I know that one apple is worth more than all the gold and diamonds in this world."

"Moo," she sighed sympathetically.

"Thanks, buddy," I answered, "but feeling bad about a mistake isn't enough. I've gotta make sure I don't make the same mistake again."

Turning to the rest of the animals, I announced, "From now on, I'm dividing the island in half. From Disappointment Hill to the eastern beach is mine. I can change it, develop it, do whatever I like with it. But from the meadow to the western claw, the island belongs to itself. I'll put everything back the way I found it, fill every hole, replant every tree, and leave nothing but footprints when I'm done."

To the cheers of "moos" and "baas," I replied, "We've gotta take care of our environment so it can take care of us."

CHAPTER 16

EVERYTHING HAS A PRICE

I didn't intend to build a whole house. All I wanted to do was move the chicken coop. I hadn't factored that structure into my original environmental proclamation, so once I started scouting for a new location, I realized my options were limited. The eastern beach was too narrow—and too crowded, when you throw in the expanding garden—so the only other alternative was the hill.

I hadn't been up there in ages, not since I was scared and starving and half nuts. Now, clad in armor, with a full belly, a rested brain, and a cache of more items than I could store, I was finally in the state of mind to accept another treasure: the view.

It was hard to believe that I used to feel such a letdown looking out over this beautiful island. The beaches, the woods, the dots of red and yellow flowers among the tans, blues, and greens. And so many greens. I'd never really noticed how the darker leaves contrasted with the lighter grass which, in turn, couldn't have been more different than the brass-tinged stalks of ripening wheat. What a sight. What a sensation.

The breeze alone was enough to give me pause. I'd been taking it for granted. Now, after spending at least half my time stuck down in the stuffy confines of the underworld, its gentle caresses were as delicious as fresh cake.

"Why didn't I come up here more often?" I called down to Moo, and then, hearing her distant reply, realized I should have been asking a much more important question. "Why don't I live here?"

As with so many of my critical decisions, this one came with a healthy dose of "duh!"

"Why am I cowering in a bunker like some kind of helpless refugee?" I asked Moo. "Mobs don't attack me indoors. Well, zombies do, but they only attack *the* doors, no matter if they're in a bunker or a house."

House.

I tingled at the idea. A proper home aboveground. Civilized. Normal.

"New priority!" I proclaimed to the animals, and got right to work mapping out the foundation.

Construction took a full four weeks, which included acquiring all the necessary materials.

At first I considered stone. All that mining had filled several chests with it. The problem was that I didn't have enough of the nicer speckled white and pink rocks for a whole house, and the dull, drab cobblestone was . . . well, dull and drab. I wanted a bright, cheery feeling that wouldn't remind me of living underground. And so I settled on birchwood, two whole forests' worth. I chopped down every single tree on the island, replanted saplings in the exact same spots, chopped them down again, and then replanted again. I hadn't forgotten to restore the land to its natural state.

Constantly replanting saplings brought up the guilty memories of causing the extinction of oak trees. "So easy," I reminded my friends halfway through my second replanting. "If I'd been as careful with oaks as I am with birch trees I could have just lived on apples."

It was Rainy, whose "baa" gave me an answer.

"Good point, kiddo," I said, planting another seedling. "If I'd preserved the oaks, I wouldn't have needed to make new tools and new discoveries. Heck, you probably wouldn't even be here."

It was a profound truth that I'd come back to many times, that problems force progress.

"No, I'm not saying it wasn't a mistake," I quickly qualified to Moo, "but mistakes can be a pretty good teacher. Maybe the best."

When I'd finished my second replanting, I had enough birchwood for the primary structure, and it was quite a structure! Twelve blocks long, twelve wide, twelve high, and divided up into four stories.

The first story was nothing but a grand entryway built right over the former site of my "HELP!" sign. Double doors opened onto a spacious room ringed by glass windows and lit by overhead lava. No joke, four blocks of molten rock encased in glass. The idea had sprung from the original reason I'd thought to build a house: the chicken coop!

I still had to figure out where to move my flock and with the hilltop gone, I was plum out of ideas. "What am I supposed to do?" I asked Moo, wishing I could scratch my head. "Make more island?"

"Moo," she answered, which could only be taken for "Why not?"

I'll say this for my mottled mate: she could bounce back ideas like sunlight off the moon.

"Why not," I repeated, rushing back to my chests full of stone.

The goal was solid, but the method took some refining. Initially I tried placing one block at a time, diving down to the southern slope of the hill. Not only did it take forever, but each plunge brought up my first memories of nearly drowning.

There's gotta be a better way, I thought after my nineteenth or twentieth dive. As is usually the case in this world, there was.

"If only," I lamented to the animals, "I could just make a whole new beach in one quick step, you know, like I did by pouring lava over water." Then correcting myself, said, "I mean water over lava."

"Baa," interrupted blackstone-colored Flint, forcing me to consider what I'd just said.

"Whoa," I breathed. "Ya think?"

More "baas" and a "moo" sealed it.

"Mistakes are the best teachers," I said, taking my empty buckets below. "Even if the mistake is a slip of the tongue."

Of all the difficult, dangerous tasks I'd accomplished on this island, making more island turned out to be a cinch. Don't ask me why the lava's safe and cool in an iron bucket, or why it's molten hot again the moment you pour it back out, or why when you pour it on water it creates cobblestone, not blackstone, but all those things happened just as I've described. Before I knew it I had a cobblestone platform jutting out from the southern shore of the hill. Not only was it big enough for a new coop, the fact that I could safely scoop the lava back up gave me another idea.

Three buckets later, I had my entryway lighting, which, by the way, illuminated a ground-level floor of blackstone. Ironically, the cooled rock had proved more difficult to obtain than its liquid variety. Eventually it took a pickaxe crafted from the last of my diamonds, but in the end I had a smooth, black, lava-lit entryway. And that was only the first floor.

One story up was my wraparound kitchen: a furnace in each corner with chests and crafting tables lining every wall. I learned that wooden slabs, the same kind that made my upper floors and ceilings, could also be used as shelves. I made eight shelves in total, two for each wall. I pictured how each would look with scrumptious, ever-fresh cakes on them, which would be infinitely more civilized than eating them off the floor.

The third floor was my grand bedroom. A double bed looked out across the carpeted floor. That's right, carpet. Experimenting with wool taught me that two blocks side-by-side got me three thin, flat carpet squares that could be laid right over an existing floor. And in five colors: the standard wool colors of black, gray, and white, *and* red and yellow, from the two types of flowers. Remember when I'd tried to eat those flowers, and holding them in my hand had gotten me the potential to make dye? And remember when I'd crafted my first bed, and the white wool had changed to a red blanket? Well, both those memories clicked together into a multicolored checkerboard carpet lining the edges of my bedroom. Not the middle, mind you; the middle was reserved for my hot tub.

You heard me.

This invention was my architectural masterpiece. Recalling how my crafting table had torched on the canyon's blackstone floor got me thinking about a safe way to transfer heat. The final product was a complicated but spectacular achievement that serviced three of the four floors.

It was the inner core of my entire structure; a transparent tower of glass, lava, glass, and water. It lit the first two floors and gave me an unheard-of luxury for the third. I couldn't believe the sensation of dipping my body into that steaming pool. What decadence! It relaxed every muscle in my body. It worked out nerves I didn't know I had. I loved my hot tub so much I even built trapdoors in the ceiling above it, so after a hard day's work I could strip off my armor and drop right in.

Did I mention the top floor was my workshop? I built it larger than the other floors—fourteen-by-fourteen—and encased it in floor-to-ceiling fences. This allowed the heat from my furnaces to be carried away by the ocean breeze.

Like the kitchen, I stacked the corners with furnaces and lined the walls with chests, crafting tables, and my inimitable anvil.

Standing on the roof allowed me to see farther beyond the horizon, which in turn gave me another idea: a watchtower.

I'd already used some of my overflowing cobblestone to build an external staircase behind the back of my house. Starting on the former space of my earthen hut, it allowed me to zip from floor to floor in no time, and without ruining the uncluttered layout of my house.

Initially I thought I'd finish at the roof, but then seeing the view from up there, and seeing I still had a ridiculous surplus of cobblestone, I looked up at the passing clouds and thought, *Why stop now?*

Up and up I went, laying a new floor every ten blocks or so to break any accidental falls, and placing torches in open windows. Those windows let in progressively colder wind. By the next morning, I could feel my teeth starting to chatter. "Last floor," I said, as the cobblestone in my pack ran out. Laying the last stone, I looked up to the square opening above and saw white. I had walked right up into a cloud.

I'm not being poetic here. I mean the tower was so tall that I was actually standing inside the white, wet mist of a moving cloud! As it slowly drifted past me, I looked down and gasped. My island was so small, just this little patch of green and brown among the endless blue. And that was the only land in sight. I was so high up that even the square edges of the horizon were visible, and yet there was nothing else but ocean.

I'm truly alone in this world, I thought, and the reaffirmation of that cold truth might have been the subconscious reason for my next and final addition to my mansion.

Like the tower, it was situated behind the house, to the right of the stairwell, and accessed through a doorway at the back of the first floor. It was a spacious room, constructed entirely of sandstone. I chose sandstone over birch for a very practical reason. It was easier to clean, and I needed this room to be as clean as possible.

After all, this was my bathroom.

To the right of the door was a sink, for washing my hands. In the rear center ceiling, I placed a trapdoor to air out all the bad smells. Directly underneath it, I placed another hatch in the floor. This was my toilet seat.

It really wasn't a seat, just a cover for the toilet, and that invention, like the sink, consisted of a water cube directly under the hatch. Unlike for the sink, however, I dug out a diagonal tunnel running all the way to the sea.

And it worked! I dropped a cube of brown earth into the water, ran down to the beach, and watched it wash out into the open ocean.

"Moo!" I called, running from the beach back up to the house. "Moo, c'mere! You gotta see this."

She snorted, clearly more interested in the patch of grass before her.

"No, for real!" I insisted. "You have *got* to see this." When she didn't respond, I pulled a stalk of ripe wheat from my belt. "Any takers?"

"Moo!" she replied, following me up the western slope of the hill. Maybe it was a little uncool to bribe her with food, but I knew she'd understand once she witnessed this achievement.

Leading her through the double doors, I waved the wheat at

my bathroom monument. "How 'bout that?" I asked, explaining how everything worked.

"Moo," she responded in a flat, euphoria-dampening tone.

"No, I know I don't need it," I admitted, "and I know I can't use it but I built it because . . ." I struggled for an answer. "Because . . . I don't know why, okay?"

I don't know.

Stopping to think about my answer forced me to admit that I didn't have one. Why had I gone through all this effort to build a room I would never use? I hadn't even thought about it during construction. I'd just gone ahead and done it. Why? And why had I been so intent on showing it off to Moo?

Was there a part of my brain that was trying to use this room for another reason? A reminder of the deeper, more uncomfortable questions I'd sworn to someday answer, but was now trying to avoid?

When you're trying to tell yourself something, listen! I should have realized that right then and there. What I shouldn't have done was try to deny the confusion bubbling up uncomfortably from my gut. What I shouldn't have done was try to change the subject. "Point is, I'm done building," I announced, feeding Moo her wheat, "and this calls for a celebration!"

Rushing up to my bedroom, I grabbed a special tool from the chest. "And what better way to celebrate than with a roast chicken dinner."

Maybe it was just timing. Maybe the hearts rising from Moo after her meal would have vanished anyway by the time I came back down with the axe. Or maybe it was an expression of her feelings, just like the long, low "moo" that followed.

"Don't start in with me again," I said, making for the door. "We had this discussion already."

"Moo," she continued, imploring me to change my mind.

"I know what I'm doing!" I snapped, heading down to the coop.

During my monthlong construction, I'd still continued to raise more fowl. Every time a wheat square ripened, every time I harvested extra seeds, I used them to grow the flock. Now I had over three dozen crammed against the straining fences.

Free food, I thought, wading into their midst, and I say "waded" because they were packed so tightly it was like trying to walk upstream. Some looked up at me as I approached, expecting, no doubt, to be fed. Even when they saw my empty hand, some continued to stare up at the falling axe.

They didn't run.

They didn't fear.

They just stood there, looking around, looking at each other, or continuing to look up at me as the iron cleaver chopped their squawking lives into loose feathers and plump pink carcasses.

I'll never forget those eyes: so small, so trusting. I'll never forget those high-pitched squawks.

There was no blood. One more quirk of this crazy world. I knew there should have been, though, remembering some buried metaphor about it being on my hands.

Finally, I was left with three baby chicks looking up at my notched blade.

"Free food," I sighed, then brought the axe down for the last time . . . on the pen's gate.

"Go on," I told the hatchlings. "You're free."

The chicks wouldn't budge. "Go on!" I yelled. "Go! Get outta here!"

They only meandered in small, lazy circles, as if the mass slaughter of their community had no effect on them.

"Okay, fine!" I barked, raising my weapon again. I chopped up the rest of the fence until there was nothing left but the cobblestone base. Only then did they casually peck over to the beach.

The cooked meat was soft and savory and it made me sick to my stomach. *So this is what guilt tastes like,* I thought between bites.

After dinner, I walked down the dusk-lit hill to my friends. At least I hoped they were still my friends. What would they think of me after what they'd seen? Was it even half as bad as what I thought of myself?

"I chose to make new lives and I chose to take them away," I said, my eyes fixed on the setting sun. "I didn't have to. I wanted to. I chose."

At that moment Moo looked silently up at me. *Did you learn?*

"I did," I said, refusing to meet her gaze. "I learned that nothing is free. Everything has a price, especially if that price is your conscience."

Satisfied, Moo looked away.

"Make no mistake," I continued, "I'm gonna cook and eat every last one of them. The only thing worse than taking their lives is wasting them. And unless I'm someday pushed to the brink of starvation with no other choices left, I swear I'll never raise my hand against another life that doesn't threaten mine."

And at that moment, Moo shuffled just a little bit closer to me, offering a forgiveness I didn't feel I deserved.

CHAPTER 17

IT'S NOT FAILURE THAT MATTERS, BUT HOW YOU RECOVER

I'd like to say that it was a nightmare that woke me in such a funk. It would have been a nice excuse. But the truth is that, just like the first time, I didn't remember anything. Even if I had, I doubt it could have competed with the horrible memories of what I'd done the day before. Still shrouded in guilt, still replaying those squawking cries, I slouched slowly downstairs, and practically collided with a creeper.

It was standing in the middle of the entryway, right in front of the open double doors, and vibrating with the hiss of a fuse.

Quick as lightning, I jumped back and off to the side, into the bathroom. The explosion was deafening: an earsplitting blast of splintering wood and shattering glass!

Unhurt, I twisted around to a sickening sight. The entryway was destroyed, all the windows gone, including the glass ceiling.

Molten lava was pouring down, covering the floor, blocking my exit. I slammed the bathroom's wooden door shut, but it promptly burst into flames. I was trapped and I was naked. I'd taken everything off before going to bed. No tools to knock out an exit, not even a spare block of cobblestone to seal the doorway. I looked up at the ventilation hatch, too high to jump through, then down to my only other option: the toilet.

As the burning door disintegrated in a flood of flaming rock, I threw open the hatch and leapt into the potty. Instantly, the current took hold and flushed me through the sewage tunnel. I plunged into the sea, shot back up to the surface, and gasped.

My house was burning, lava sparks igniting wood. The expression "spreading like wildfire" suddenly took on new meaning as fresh planks caught in a chain reaction that threatened to consume the entire mansion.

Was there some way, *any* way, to smother the flames? Maybe a bucket of water? But all my buckets and reserve iron were either in the entryway or up in the workshop.

What to do? What to *do*!? The flames rose and spread, eating my beautiful home like a flickering, ravenous beast, and leaving, like the discarded bones of a meal, fireproof objects suspended in mid-air. Windows, chests, furnaces, all surrounded by cubes of flowing lava.

The hill was now a volcano. Blazing liquid oozed down the eastern slope before me, demolishing my precious garden. And on the western slope . . .

"Baa!"

THE ANIMALS!

Heart racing, I swam around to the meadow. The red river was coming, destroying everything in its path. Soon it would reach the open field and then the forest. The trees! All that wood! Where were my . . .

I could see the cow and sheep family, all still grazing as if nothing were wrong.

"Run!" I shouted. "Go, go, go, go!"

They continued munching, oblivious to their peril.

"Don't you see it!?" I hollered, pointing to the roiling tide. "You gotta get outta here!"

They glanced at me dimly as if this were just another monologue.

I had to stop the lava.

Build a wall? Nothing to build with . . .

DIG!

Frantically, I tore into the earth with my bare hands, trying to cut a trench between my friends and a fiery fate. Blocks of earth flew into my belt as the lava reached the meadow; another two squares and it would be on me. Scorching my hair, baking my face.

Popping, bubbling, laughing heat. *Here I come.*

Made it! I jumped out of the trench just a half step ahead of the flaming flood. The ditch filled and held, and for a second, I thought I'd saved the day. Then a spark popped from the barrier onto my skin. Recoiling from the sting, I backed right into Rainy.

"Hey, what are you—" I began, but stopped as the sheep ambled right past me.

"NO!" I shouted pushing it back. It was like the lamb couldn't see the trench, didn't know that certain death was only a few steps away. "Get back!" I roared, shoving the deluded animal.

"Help me save your baby!" I shouted to its black and white parents. In a gut-punch of irony, I saw that the parents were also casually meandering over.

"What's wrong with you!?" I yelled, trying to jostle them back. I was just pushing Cloud into the tree line when a sound turned my stomach to stone.

"Moo."

Eyes flicking across the meadow, I saw my cow, my con-science, my best friend in the whole world, on her way to a flam-ing execution.

"Moo!" I screamed, sprinting over to bodily bounce her away. "Please, you gotta understand!" I begged. "You're gonna die! Don't you get it!? You're gonna die!"

She wouldn't listen, wouldn't stop.

"Please, Moo!" I pleaded, racing back and forth between her and the sheep. "Please, please, just listen to me! All of you, listen! Pleeease!"

At that moment I heard a sickening "B'geck!" and turned to see one of the chickens stepping into the fire-filled trench. A bloom of orange and red, a flash of feathers and cooked carcass, and then it was all gone.

"Look!" I screeched through hysterical tears. "Don't you see!?"

They didn't. Something in their brains, in the rules of this world. A fatal blind spot. A cruel joke.

"Stop it, Moo!" I thundered. "You stupid, bloody hamburger!" My fist shot out, socking her square in the face.

With a flashing red "moo!" she ran from the flames.

"I'm sorry," I cried, punching the sheep away. "I had to!"

They ran to the safety of the trees, stopped, and, to my throat-closing horror, began slowly walking back. I couldn't keep punching them forever. Another blow might kill them. And I couldn't keep pushing all of them back. Eventually one, or maybe all, would end up fried in the ditch.

I had to extinguish the source. I *had* to cool that lava!

Looking up at the hill, I saw my one slim ray of hope: the rest of the hot tub, including the water, still sat above the fiery gusher. If I could just smash the glass between the water and the lava below it . . . but how to get there? The stone tower was still standing. Maybe I could use the dirt blocks in my hand to make a bridge.

I took off running for the southern slope, the one spot that still seemed clear. I tore up the incline as fast as my rectangular legs could carry me, then stopped as if hitting an invisible wall.

From the summit of the hill I could now see that a seething river lay between me and the tower. Worse still, lava was actually surging into the tower itself so even if I got there, I'd still be cooking myself for dinner.

A sudden, crazy idea sprang from the paltry dirt cubes in my hand. It was a reckless plan, a hopeless gamble, and when it came to self-preservation, a completely unnecessary risk.

But maybe it was a different kind of self-preservation: preservation of the soul. Losing my friends would drive me crazy, especially knowing that it had all been my fault. And maybe, just maybe, if I risked my life to save them, it could be some slight redemption for the mass slaughter of so many others.

None of this was conscious. There was no rational decision chain. At the moment, all I could think about was getting up to that water. I sprinted over to the edge of the stream, placing my first dirt block within its molten mass.

I'd pictured building a raised path all the way to tower, but simple math told me I didn't have enough dirt. I'd have to stagger them every other square and jump perilously from one to the other. I hopped up onto the first block, then the second block; then turning back to the first, tried to punch it back up. I thought if I could collect the dirt behind me, I could remake it into a bridge from the tower to the hot tub.

I thought wrong. No sooner had the earthen cube been released from the floor when it incinerated in the lava's heat. There wasn't time to reconsider. Every moment brought my friends closer to death.

Hop, skip, jump, all the while knowing one mistake would be my last. If I hadn't been grateful enough for the superpower of long-range reach in the past, I certainly was now.

Hop. Place. Skip. Place. Jump.

I made it to within a few steps of the tower and placed the last few blocks at its entrance. The lava began to drain, but not fast enough.

Wait till it's safe. Just a few more seconds.

Then, from the meadow, a plaintive "moo."

Mind flashing with the image of that burnt chicken, and with that image morphing into a burning steak, I sprang into the tower.

Just one thin mini-cube layer of lava. That's all it took to set me alight. With flame-clouded vision, and the agonizing smell of my own roasting meat, I charged up three flights of stairs.

The tub, four blue cubes across from my open doorway. An island of water in an ocean of fire.

One chance. Slim chance. To miss and fall . . .

"Moo."

She was almost to the trench, another few steps and . . .

"Yaaaaaa!" I launched, trailing smoke and cinders. Arcing up . . . leveling off . . . down . . . down . . . Time slowed. Eternity in flight. Too long? Too short!

Miss!

Splash!

Cool, quenching relief.

Hit!

"Moo!"

Don't rest! Don't stop!

Bare, burnt fists smashed at the glass floor.

Crack!

Water rushed out, smothering the lava, turning it to blackstone, but blocking it from reaching the hill!

Keep going!

I shattered the clear walls and, once again, was flushed away.

Carried down the hill on a ramp of new, steaming cobblestone, I landed softly in the trench, and right at the feet of my friend.

"Moo." Thank you.

But I didn't notice her, or the other saved animals, or anything else except the image of what had once been my beautiful home. Nothing was left standing but a suspended waterfall in a skeleton of hanging windows. It was all gone; all of my accomplishments, all of my work. All of that time and energy and thought and wealth. All gone.

And what did I feel at that moment?

Nothing.

I was numb. No anger, no grief; I was as empty as the ruined shell before me.

Failure.

The word closed in like nightfall. I'd failed. I'd ruined everything.

I was a failure.

I don't know how long I watched the ruins. I'm guessing the better part of the day. I didn't feel the hunger or the half-healed wounds. I didn't feel the nudges of my friends, didn't hear their calls. I didn't want to listen, or feel, or think, or care. I didn't want to *be*.

The sun set, warm rays fading to evening chills. I didn't move. Still and silent. Detached. Over.

"Guuuggg!"

The blow struck me hard in the back of the head, knocking me literally forward and figuratively back into the here and now. Spinning, I saw the looming ghoul, and without thinking, I said, "Thank you."

Running into my observation bubble, now nearly submerged in the waterfall, I slammed the door behind me. The zombie didn't follow. It couldn't. Through the window I watched it enter the trench, hit the water, try to push through, and get knocked back in over and over again.

"You just keep going," I said through the glass. "You'll never stop."

I thought of that first night, cowering in a pitch-black hole, hunger gnawing at my insides while an undead predator lurked within arm's reach. How far had I come since that vulnerable, terrifying ordeal? Even now, with the ruins of my home still smoking on the hill above me, I could not deny my progress. I was safe in my well-lit bunker, with all the hard-won skills I needed to completely rebuild my life.

And I would rebuild.

That night, locking eyes with the indomitable zombie, I told him, "You don't stop, and neither will I. I'll be back tomorrow. I'll craft new tools, plant new crops, build a new house, and come out of this experience stronger and smarter!"

The ghoul gurgled back.

I said, "Thank you for knocking some sense into me. Thank you for making me see that it's not failure that matters, but how you recover from it."

CHAPTER 18

WHEN TRYING TO TELL YOURSELF SOMETHING, *LISTEN!*

"Ya know," I said to my friends the next morning, "losing that house might be one of the best things that's ever happened to me on this island."

"Baa," said Rainy.

"Yes, really," I continued, "'cause it just added another 'P' to my Way."

The lamb looked at me quizzically.

"Sorry," I said. "You weren't born yet when I discovered the Five P's: Planning, Preparing, Prioritizing, Practice, and Patience. And now"—I held up a theatrical fist—"*Perseverance,* which is just a fancy way of repeating my first lesson of not giving up! But when you put it with the other P's, it makes a cube!"

At that point they all turned away.

"How fitting," I told their butts, "in more ways than one. 'Cause if you laid all these P's out on the ground, you could fold them up into a cube, which is what this whole world's made of." I took a moment to let this profound epiphany sink in, and took from their munching sounds that they were as impressed with me as I was with myself.

"The Way of the Cube," I said grandly, striding among them with outstretched hands, "and the perfect philosophy for my next project."

"Baa," said Cloud.

"Oh no," I told my pale companion, "not a new house, not yet. Not before finally tackling the reason I lost the first one."

Looking up at the burned-out, waterfall-filled ruin on the hill, I asked, "How long ago did I realize that torchlight prevents mob spawns? And how many times did I plan to light the whole island? But I never did it because I got distracted by other projects, and, to be honest, it seemed boring. And look at the price I paid for it. No more. That house-destroying creeper taught me yet another priceless life lesson: Ne—"

Turning back toward my friends, I saw that they'd all walked away in the middle of my monologue.

"Never put off the boring-but-important chores!" I shouted after their retreating forms.

And so I went straight to work on lighting up my island. I used up all my coal and most of my wood to make enough torches to carpet the land. I placed them on trees, on grass, on the beaches, even in the middle of the lagoon on a single column of cobblestone. I wasn't taking any chances.

Yes, I know, I'd promised to leave that part of the island exactly as I found it, but I reasoned that if I didn't mob-proof the environment with torches, then I risked damaging it further with more mob attacks. Sometimes you have to compromise an ideal in order to save it.

I'm glad I did.

"Not one mob," I said to Moo, standing in the midnight meadow, watching the torches blend with the stars. "Not a single spawn from one end of the island to the other."

"Moo," she answered agreeably. I looked up to the stars on their slow, straight journey west. "I could stare at them all night." And then on that thought, I added, "In fact, why do I need a house anymore?" I imagined my bed on the bare summit of the hill, with only the stars for cover. "The island's safe and the temperature's always mild. Why do I need a roof over my head?"

And at that moment—and this really happened—it began to rain. And not those little drizzly showers that came every now and then. This was a full-blown storm, with ground-shaking thunder and cracks of white lightning.

"That's why," I said, sheltering under a tree with Moo.

Just thinking about being struck made me shiver. As much as I'd like to sleep out under the stars, I'd also need a roof over my head.

And it wouldn't be a wooden roof this time. In fact, the whole structure would be fireproof. Remember that story of the three pigs? I did, right down to the exact detail of using bricks.

No reason substance can't have style, right? I found that bricks were just as strong as cobblestone, and they also looked really nice.

I dug up all the clay from the lagoon's underwater pits, but after replacing the bottom layers with sand, I put that top layer right back in order to restore its natural beauty. I was lucky to have enough clay to make plenty of bricks for a cozy cottage.

I guess I won't have to describe what the house looks like to you. Unless, of course, you're reading a copy of this story or the original's been moved somewhere else. I'm gonna assume it's in the same place, though, and that you've seen the smaller, C-shaped building that mirrors the natural form of the island.

You've seen the kitchen and workshop wings on the first floor, the bedroom and walk-in closets on the second. You've seen the iron front door and the two trapdoors on each wing for ventilation, as well as the iron-bar windows I have at the north and south walls of each upper floor. Doesn't that sea breeze feel good?

You've seen that I learned how to make a clay flower pot that

I left next to my bed, and an armor stand in the closet. And you've seen that I figured out how to stain glass blocks in the ceiling and make proper, thin, elegant windowpanes downstairs.

Most important, though, you've seen the paintings.

Those came about when I was making a new bed. *Now that I'm not using flammable wool for carpeting anymore*, I thought, *why not mess around a little with it and see if I can come up with anything else?*

And I did. A mix of sticks and wool got me the image of a blank white canvas stretched in a wooden frame. It was only when I grabbed it that the real bizarreness began. Experience suggested that this object belonged on the wall, and when I placed it on the naked bricks, the surface suddenly filled with brilliantly colored mini-squares! The sheer surprise made me back up a few steps, and that was when I saw a clear pattern.

It was a human figure from my world, tall and rounded, with black clothes and reddish hair, standing on a mountain top, looking over a white landscape. "Whoa . . ." I breathed, feeling truly gobsmacked. This was a whole new level of crafting. Not the basic, generic items like a pickaxe or a bed. This was a clear, specific, unique image.

"How?" I asked aloud. How had this world decided on what would fill the canvas?

I punched up the painting, trying to examine it closer. The image went blank. I placed it back on the wall, and saw something completely different. Not only had the frame changed shape, but the picture now appeared to be two black and white figures reaching for each other.

"Wha . . ." I whispered, and removed it again. The third time, it kept the same horizontal frame but changed the image to a very recognizable creeper. And that's when the theory formed. Was the world choosing these images or was I? The first two subjects were real paintings from my world. In fact the very first painting, the man on the mountaintop, had been reproduced on the cover of a book I'd once read, something about a man creating a monster. Was this world somehow channeling my memories? Was this the key to remembering who I was?

Leaving the creeper painting up as a fitting reminder to always close the door, I got to work on another frame, and placed it on the wall in my bedroom.

What else will I remember? I thought.

I gaped at the painting that appeared. At first I didn't think it came from either world. The subject was of a man, I think, with yellow skin, a red shirt, blue pants, and a triangular, blue and red hat. At first his crude outline looked squarish, but the thin lines just didn't match up with this world.

And then it hit me.

"You're King Graham," I said to the picture, "from the computer game King's Quest."

Computers.

I'd thought a lot about the conveniences of my world: refrigeration, microwave ovens, TV, and AC. All of them were in reference to making my life here more comfortable. But computers were different. They didn't just help my life, they were my life.

That's why I don't know how to fish, or cook, or tend a garden. I've spent my life in front of a screen . . .

But who did that life belong to?

Stepping out of the house, I didn't think about where I was going, or notice that it'd begun to drizzle. I didn't even realize that I'd begun humming a song from my world, the same one I'd remembered that horrible first night on the island.

"You may find yourself," I said aloud, meandering almost dreamily down the hill. As before, I couldn't recall all the lyrics. It was like trying to listen to a neighbor's radio through a wall. All I could come up with was that same one from before.

"And you may ask yourself," I sang to Moo. "Well, how did I get here?" And then, looking down at my friend, asked, "And *why* am I here?"

It hadn't dawned on me up until that moment that there might be a conscious reason for my entry into this bizarre, blocky world. I'd either been too busy or, let's be honest, too unwilling to even think that something, someone, had intentionally taken me.

"If there's a reason for me being here," I asked Moo, "then what is it?"

Just saying it out loud made me uncomfortable. I could feel my neck muscles tighten, my stomach churn, and any peace I'd rebuilt with the new house evaporate like dead-zombie smoke.

Sensing my growing discomfort, Moo ventured a questing "moo."

"I don't know," I answered, at that moment despising those three terrifying words. "I don't know why asking these questions is making me feel so . . . small and scared? I mean, haven't I been working toward answering them all along? Wasn't that the reason for the grand strategy? The whole point of nailing down food, shelter, and safety was to give me the space to concentrate on the really big questions, and now that I've done all that, now that the moment's here . . ."

I suddenly felt like I was standing on a cliff, like when I'd almost fallen into the lava of the underground canyon. And just like during that terrifying ordeal, I backed way up into safety.

"Now that the moment's here," I said, pivoting into desperate denial, "I deserve to enjoy it! Right?"

Moo just looked at me.

"After all," I continued, "those questions'll still be here tomorrow, or next week, right? I'm entitled to take a moment to smell the flowers, or enjoy the sunset." And looking out at the appropriately setting sun, I concluded with "Which is the perfect time to test my new hot tub."

Walking back to the house, I could swear Moo's call sounded like "Wait, we gotta talk about this."

"Sorry," I said, practically skipping away. "Time for some me-time."

I'd rebuilt my hot-water luxury over the foundation of my former chicken coop. Not only was it a heck of a lot safer than keeping live lava in the house, but the ocean breeze, and now the rain, made it a perfect location.

Soaking in the steaming water, watching the sun dip between the clouds and the sea, I tried to enjoy this near-perfect moment. But it wasn't absolutely perfect; the questions had followed me into the tub.

Who? Where? Why?

I tried to close my eyes, to focus on the breeze and the rain. I tried concentrating on the chores of the next morning, like tending the replanted garden and repairing my armor and tools. I tried to imagine some new decorations like rows of flowers or maybe a fountain.

Nothing worked. Questions, I realized, don't stay put; you can't just walk away from them.

Not that I didn't try. For the second time in ten minutes, I got up and left. "Time for bed," I told myself, even though sunset had become my favorite time of day. I walked up to the house, ready to spend my first night in my newly finished masterpiece. I hoped that a good night's sleep and a morning of comforting routine would keep me focused on the here and now.

That's when I noticed the torches, or lack thereof. I only had one on the top floor and one on the bottom. I'd used all the others to light the island.

"Oh that's bad," I said, shaking my head dramatically. "That's really bad."

Looking out through the bars of my bedroom window, I called down to Moo, "See that? Too dark! I gotta get more torches and more coal. I gotta get mining again."

"Moo," came an answer that I took as "You know you're just making up excuses."

"No, seriously," I countered. "What if one torch isn't enough to keep mobs from spawning?"

Again came a long, scolding, will-you-just-deal-with-what's-bothering-you-already "moo."

"Hold that thought," I said, reaching for my armor and tools. "We'll talk later."

Pickaxe in hand, sword and shield on my belt, and a healthy ration of bread and carrots in my pack, I made my way back down below the earth.

Surveying the underground canyon made me realize how thoroughly mined-out it was. Glittering ore caches had been replaced by gaping holes. The walls actually looked like some hungry creature had taken huge bites out of them, which I guess wasn't that far from the truth.

The side tunnels had been equally ravaged. Previously dark tubes were now well-lit passageways. And, of course, the well-lit part was what I didn't want to think about. If I was really after coal for torches, I could have grabbed some ready-made ones right off the walls around me.

For a moment, I seriously considered doing just that: taking a few torches, heading back home, and trying to find another way to avoid answering those really big questions.

"Gaaahhh."

The groan actually brought a smile to my flat face.

"Gaaahhh."

Somewhere down here, in some dark spot I'd somehow missed, was a distracting, delaying dead guy.

Drawing my sword I looked in every direction. I couldn't see anything at first.

"Gaaahhh!" These groans sounded slightly different than usual, higher pitched. I listened carefully, thinking maybe it was a trick of the canyon. And then something came flying out of the darkness.

I blanched as a miniature, halfling, baby zombie raced toward me from a small hole in the wall. And when I say raced, I mean *raced*. This little imp was fast! Before I could even raise Flash it'd crashed into me like a freight train. Flying back, I barely uttered a startled "oof" before it struck me a second time.

And it wasn't just fast, it was tough. I don't know how many times I'd swung before Flash finally smoked it.

"What the what!?" I croaked, wolfing down food to heal the pain. Peering into the half-zie's hiding spot, I couldn't make out any treasure. No coal, iron, or anything of value. What this opening did present, however, was a chance to pretend that I actually cared about exploring.

I picked away a me-sized opening and stepped cautiously through. I raised my shield, waiting for the inevitable arrow. It didn't come. I waited a few extra moments, listening for the groan of a zombie or the hiss of a spider. Nothing but silence.

Stepping gingerly forward, I thought I saw an object in the light of the tunnel's entrance.

It looked like a plant, or at least something plantlike, growing right out of the rock floor. Stepping closer, I could make out three short, stubby, tan-colored shrubs. My foot must have gotten too close to one, because it popped off the stone floor and up into my belt. Looking closer, I could see it was a mushroom.

"Ew," I grimaced, thinking that either they were poisonous or would make me see long-dead rock stars. What a change from my earlier time of starvation when I would have literally killed for one.

That's when I noticed the other light.

I figured it had to be another lava pit, although the tunnel ahead was getting colder with each step. Guard up, weapon ready, I marched the last few paces to a sharp descent in the tunnel.

What I saw took my breath away. At the bottom of a rough, steep slope was a torch—not one of mine—attached to a wooden frame.

"I'm not alone!" I exclaimed, ironically hearing only my own echo in reply. So many images flashed before my mind: the boots I'd pulled out of the ocean, the questions about what lay beyond the horizon, and, with a sudden, sharp sense of danger, the witch.

What if this was its home? What if there were more of them?

Balancing between verve and vigilance, I crept to the bottom of the slope and stared in pure shock down the length of an artificial mineshaft. The walls had been carefully scraped out into a neat four-by-four pattern. Every few steps, the ceiling was supported by wooden crossbeams set on double-high fence posts. I couldn't tell how far back the tunnel went. Darkness blotted out anything beyond a few dozen paces.

Who made this? I wondered. *And when? And where are they?* My head was spinning with questions.

Had my island once been inhabited? Had there been another individual like me, or a group of people who had come here, built this, then left? If so, where was the surface evidence, like structures and homes? Had the original miners decided to restore the entire island to its natural state before leaving? If so, why hadn't they taken all the other minerals I'd found up until this point?

Maybe they'd taken as much as they needed, or—my pulse raced—maybe the island hadn't been their starting point, but their ending! Maybe this mining tunnel ran under the ocean and out to reality, or a new world, or a different island, at the very least.

I thought about calling out to whoever might still be here, but then reasoned that they might also be hostile.

Just because someone looks like you doesn't make them a friend.

Once again I came back to the theory of a witch's lair, and decided not to advertise my presence.

I noticed that the woodblocks and fence posts were oak, not birch, and since the former had been rarer up on my island before I, well, caused their extinction, maybe all this had been brought in from someplace else.

I placed a torch farther down the wall and spied another peculiarity in the distance. There were sections of wood and metal crafted to make some kind of track. I followed it hesitantly, placing torches every few steps and listening for any nearby sounds.

I passed caches of embedded coal, iron, and redstone, which I promised to dig out later. I also passed several blocks of spider webs in the upper corners of the shaft. This last observation sent my anxiety to full alert. *Maybe they've been spun by some harmless little species about the size of a crabupine. Or maybe their bigger cousins are to blame.*

Still following the track, I saw that the shaft split left and right. I looked left, saw nothing but blackness, looked right, and saw what looked like a metal box.

Getting closer, I saw that it wasn't a box but a wheeled cart that held a standard wooden storage chest. Opening the lid, I found a worn iron pickaxe and something that positively blew my mind.

It wasn't that it was crafted of diamonds, it wasn't that the diamonds had been crafted into armor, it was that the armor had been crafted for something that wasn't human! At first glance, this large protective cover seemed to be made for a four-legged animal. A cow? A sheep? Why would anyone want to protect animals that were ignored by mobs?

Maybe it's protection against another monster I haven't encountered yet, I mused, examining the glittering cover. *Or maybe it's the animal, not the monster, that I haven't encountered.*

If the second theory was true, then it bolstered my original notion that these materials were coming from someplace beyond my island.

Should I head back up to the surface to try this suit on my animal friends, or should I press on?

CLICKETY-CLACK.

There was my answer.

Three arrows—yes, *three*—came whistling from the dark to bury themselves in my ironclad chest.

I winced, turning to run down the tunnel. Like that very first underground battle. I turned a corner and waited for my pursuers to show.

CLICK.

CLICK.

CLICK.

I could hear three pairs of bony feet, although it didn't seem possible. One, maybe two, but I'd never come across that many.

You're in for it, I told myself, and I surely was. No chance for a shield-and-strike maneuver here. No way to avoid looking like a wounded hedgehog.

As the trio of archers came around the corner, I laid in with flashing, diamond-edged determination. You don't want to know how many arrows stuck out of my body by the end. I sure don't want to remember it. It was enough to devour the rest of my food and send me straight back up to the surface.

"Guys," I called to my four-legged posse. "This fit any of you?"

I took special care to hold up the diamond armor to both Moo and the sheep. Neither would accept it.

"So, what do you think it's for?" I asked them. "A deer? A horse? A water buffalo?" The middle one made the most sense, as I'd seen pictures of armored horses from my world's "Age of Dumbness." "I guess the specific animal isn't as important," I told Moo, "as the fact that there has to be other land out there." I glanced out at the horizon, feeling my insides tighten again.

"Or maybe not," I chirped, hopping back on the denial express. "This island could be a mountaintop on a world that flooded. Wasn't there a career-killing movie about that?"

The animals all stared at me.

"Whatever," I said, and headed back for the hill. "Point is, I gotta get back down there. Who knows what I'm gonna find."

I still wasn't ready to listen to what my subconscious was trying to tell me.

CHAPTER 19

BOOKS MAKE THE WORLD BIGGER

My second expedition into the mineshaft ended almost as quickly as it started. I must have been down there for only a few minutes before I found another one of those minecarts. You don't need to hear about the couple of zombies on the way. Moan, chop, poof—you get it.

What matters is what I found in the minecart's chest. And I don't mean the few pinches of redstone, or the loaf of bread that still tasted fresh after, what, a thousand years?

What sent me racing back up to the surface were the two collections of seeds. Neither looked anything like the standard, bright green wheat seeds I'd gotten so used to. The first bunch were small and black, while the seeds in the other bunch were lighter and just a little bit bigger.

In no time I was back at my garden, digging out whole new rows and scraping off the first square with my hoe. No sooner had they both gone in than I saw how different they'd be.

Wheat, even carrots, both came up in multiple shoots. Not these. Both had just one thick, green seedling.

It almost made me laugh to think that, a few months ago, I would have spent days just watching and waiting. Not now. Not with my stockpile of skeleton bone meal.

I sprinkled three pinches on the first one and watched the little sprout rise into a brownish-green, waist-high plant. It didn't have any leaves, or fruit, or anything that I could harvest. And so, since I had two more seeds in reserve, I tried harvesting the stem itself.

Maybe this is some whole new kind of food, I thought. *Something that isn't just a squarish version of what I found in my world. Or maybe it is something I would recognize, but only after I —*

My musings ended when a couple punches completely obliterated the root.

"Bing-bang-boom," I said sarcastically, and began the process of replanting and refertilizing the next handful of seeds.

This time, however, I waited patiently. I paced a little, checked on the other garden crops, harvested some wheat and carrots, and then came back to the same, stubborn little plant.

"Okay, fine," I told it. "I'm gonna go repair my armor or something. And when I get back, maybe I'll bring Moo and see if you look good to her."

As if to answer, the shrub or vine or whatever it was suddenly bent on its side, burdened with a giant, square, light-and-dark-green-striped fruit. "Now, that's a little more like it," I said, punching up the suspiciously familiar cube.

As soon as it was in my hand, the fruit separated into six slices. Inside its thick, green crust was a crunchy, pink, instantly recognizable flesh. If you've never had watermelon before, you do *not* know what you're missing.

"Mm-mm-mm," I groaned between bites, psyched to have yet another addition to my growing banquet.

"How about you?" I asked the other mystery vine between bites. "Whatchoo got?"

What I got, at least for the moment, was nothing. "Suit yourself," I told it. "We'll talk when I get back."

Before returning to the mineshaft, I replanted the other watermelon seeds. Leaving a long row of four vines and one row of the yet-to-be-identified stem, I headed back down with dreams of new discoveries.

This time, however, my findings weren't completely positive.

I was heading down the tunnel past the second looted mine-cart when three more arrows slammed into my hip.

"Again!?" I yelped, turning to confront another trio of skeletons. This time, instead of trying to ambush my attackers, I pulled back around the corner and sealed up the space between support beams with extra cobblestone.

"We're not done," I said, hatching a new plan.

Since mining had become second nature, I thought about digging around to the other side, breaking out behind them, and using the element of surprise to snag another load of clacking fertilizer.

It turned out to be a total surprise, but not for them. I didn't get very far before breaking through into a cobblestone chamber and coming face-to-fleshless-face with another pair of skeletons. There was no time for well-rehearsed sword-and-shield combat, no time to do anything except rush right past my attackers and seal the room's proper entrance before their three buddies could arrive. Taking a few not-so-fun arrows in the back, I threw down some torches, then threw down with the clicking killers.

Gathering up their remains, I gawked at the bizarre chamber I'd stumbled into. A strange little fire, encased in a strange little cage, burned in the center of the room. It threw no light or heat, and if I hadn't been so distracted by the storage chests behind it, I might have noticed the little object twirling within the flames.

But I went to the chests first and, uttering an exultant "Score,"

I reached out to open them. "OW!" I belted, as an arrow struck me between the shoulder blades.

Swinging as I spun, I caught a skeleton standing right behind me. "What the . . ." I began, wondering how one could have followed me through my tunnel. How else could one have gotten in, right?

No sooner had I raised my shield than an arrow THOCKED off its surface, and then, to my happy astonishment, ricocheted into the skeleton's chest.

"Aw, will ya look at that," I said, realizing I now had a new combat tactic. If you've never tried a Bonehead Bounce, as I now call it, know that it takes a lot of skill. First, you've gotta get real close. Second, you've gotta aim your shield just right. But when you do, there's nothing more fun than watching a shooter shoot itself. I completely forgot to wonder how the poor sap had appeared in the room with me.

Because that's exactly what happened. It just appeared. I was still ping-ponging arrows back to the first archer—and coming up with all kinds of witty comments after each shot, I might add—when suddenly a second archer poofed right into existence next to it.

And that's when things got serious. Bonehead Bounces only work with one shooter, as I quickly, and painfully, learned. Taking arrows in the shoulder, chest, and leg, I lowered my shield long enough for Flash's diamond blade to claim two of its three victims.

The battle's third and final kill was the spawner. That's what I call the caged fire sitting in the middle of the room.

I should have suspected that this weird little device was a monster factory. I should have noticed that the thing spinning in the flames was a miniature skeleton. "Idiot," I said aloud, trying not to beat up on myself. *Don't dwell on your mistakes, learn from them.*

Unfortunately in this scenario, what I'd now learned made me feel even worse. I had a new threat to deal with, a curveball that totally demolished my ironclad theory of mobs only spawning in darkness. If there were more of these monster factories around, churning out skeletons and zombies and squads of silent, explosive creepers . . .

It was enough to make me want to seal up the room, the mineshaft, and turn my back on this whole new underground realm.

Right after I loot these last two chests.

At first I found a gray, thin disc about the size of my hand. *Too bad there's nothing to play it on,* I thought, opening the second chest.

"A book!"

And not just any book, a manual. A technical instruction guide!

Up until that moment, my self-education had crawled like a snail. Observation, experimentation, and lucky, or sometimes dangerous, accidents, had been my process. No more. Within those delicate pages I found ready-made teachings just waiting to be absorbed. Opening the leather-bound volume felt like trying on a pair of wings, and reading its contents made my mind soar!

Without questioning why the words were written in my language—or, for that matter, what my language actually was—I flew back up to the surface, into my house, and into this new tome's teachings.

"I found a book!" I shouted to my friends, stepping out onto the front porch of my house. I read aloud from *The Book of Music* and taught my animal pals how to make both a jukebox to play the record I'd found, and note blocks to compose original tunes.

Okay, so maybe it wasn't the most useful information. The music didn't really deserve the name. I don't know what my tastes were back home, but this sterile, repetitive noise was about as pleasing as zombie flesh.

And as far as constructing note blocks, well, guess I could have turned my old bunker into a studio. But why do that now when there might be other books, with more useful knowledge, just waiting for me down there?

That's why I made another beeline for the mineshaft, my steps giddy with dreams of mental wealth. Given my first three forays, I think I expected to just trip over a library. That didn't happen, of course, but after exploring a few new tunnels, I turned a corner and let out a long, echoing "whoa . . ."

The shaft opened onto a cavern that made the first natural canyon seem like a ditch. It wasn't only vast, it was developed! Mineshafts led everywhere, with wooden bridges crisscrossing the open air. I could hear the rush of several waterfalls and see the glimmer of a few distant torches, as well as the glow of a faraway lava pond.

I could also see another light, which turned out to be a pair of thin purple eyes. The creature was tall, at least twice my height, and so black I almost missed it. It was down at the bottom of the canyon, above the bridge. Not the easiest shot to make, but with gravity on my side . . .

I drew my bow, lined up my shot, then paused.

Just because someone looks like you doesn't automatically make them a friend.

Remembering that old lesson mirrored a new one.

And just because someone doesn't *look like you doesn't automatically make them an enemy.*

For all I knew, this place was this creature's home, and it might have more answers than all the books I might find.

"Risk and reward," I said, lowering my bow and starting down to the bottom of the chasm. Ironically, that's when I found another chest, with a new book entitled *Wildlife*. I didn't read it right then, although I really wish I had.

Shoving the volume into my pack, I crept to within a dozen blocks of the tall dark stranger. I thought I was being safe, since I was far enough away to get off a few arrows before it reached me. I also thought, since it hadn't yet turned in my direction like a regular mob, that maybe it didn't see me as a threat.

Never assume anything. But I did.

"Hello," I called, hands resting on my bow. It didn't turn. I could see something in its long, thin arms: a block of stone?

"Hello?" I called again. No response.

I was about to step closer when the creature just happened to turn in my direction. Our eyes met.

"GHAAA!"

A chilling rasp. Blinding speed. And I really mean blinding! One minute it was far away and the next, WHOOSH, right in my face, knocking me back, bending armor and cracking ribs.

The breath rushed out of my lungs and my bow flew from my hand.

"GHAAA!" it rasped again with another near-fatal blow.

There wasn't time to do anything but bolt. I tore across the chasm floor, aiming for the nearest light. A torch at a nearby mineshaft.

Another blow, another raspy scream, and I was through. Nearly dead, and shaken to the core, but saved by the ceiling crossbeam that wouldn't let the tall super-beast enter.

Dazed and confounded, I asked, "What did I say? What did I do?"

"GHAAA," the being answered, butting up against the beam.

"This?" I asked, holding up the book. "Did I steal your book?"

"GHAAAA!"

"Here," I said, dropping the book as close to it as I could. "Take it!"

But it didn't take the book, or calm down.

"What then?" I asked, stretching out to retrieve the manual. "What's the problem?" And as I backed away, I asked, "What are you?"

"They're called Endermen," I told Moo when I made it back up to the surface, holding up the *Wildlife* guide. "But it doesn't explain much," I continued. "Except that they're neutral."

"Moo," replied Moo, supping on grass while I snacked on a pumpkin pie. Oh yeah, I found another book on the way back up, and this one was entitled *Food*. Turns out the mystery vine produced pumpkins, and the third book showed me what to do with them.

"I'm not s'posed to look them in the eye," I continued between bites of sweet pumpkiny goodness. "That's apparently what set it off. Some kind of custom that I didn't follow, maybe? And what I thought was it running real fast was actually teleporting."

Reading on, I said, "There's more here I don't understand about endermites and enderpearls, whatever those are, and some really cryptic stuff about Endermen building the world. Don't ask because I don't know, but it must have had something to do with the block of stone it was holding."

Setting the book down, I mused, "They couldn't have made the mineshafts for themselves because that one couldn't fit, and they couldn't have written this book because the book refers to them as 'they' instead of 'us.' But then why . . ."

There was that accursed word again. *Why?*

"Doesn't matter," I said dismissively, avoiding my confusion and discomfort. "I know what I need to know: don't look 'em in the eye, don't mess with 'em, and they won't mess with you. Moving on."

Skipping to the more familiar chapters, I said, "Lotta animals in this world." Then, catching myself, I added, "Or at least there used to be before the continent sank into the ocean."

"Baa," scoffed Cloud, failing to dent my denial.

"Yeah, it is sad," I said, reading on. "All those ocelots and wolves I'll never see. The armor I found was for horses, by the way, and pigs. You know you used to be able to ride a pig in this world? Steering with a carrot on a fishing rod. Go figure."

After another page, I said, "You can catch fish in any body of water." I glanced at the nearby chickens and, ignoring the stab of regret in my chest, said, "Not that I'll ever need to."

I browsed the parts about mobs, breezing through all the usual suspects. Turns out the crabupines are actually called "silverfish," like that makes any sense.

"You can actually make wool from a bunch of collected spiderwebs," I said, then to the sheep, added with a laugh, "not that I'll ever need to." I assumed I already knew what there was to know about most mobs. And so when it came to cave spiders, I assumed they were just a smaller, less dangerous version of the big kind.

Never assume anything.

I know now, though I didn't at the time, that I was reading selectively. Any section that made me feel safer, smarter, or more powerful, I read. Anything that brought up scary questions, I ignored. I guess, looking back, I wasn't much different from so many other people in my world, the kind who wouldn't read some books, or cut out certain parts, or even burned them, because of how the words inside made them feel. I didn't want to admit how I felt reading about new lands and creatures that might very well exist beyond my narrow horizon. It brought me back to the memory of pulling those old leather boots out of the ocean, and how I'd suddenly felt a whole lot smaller. That's why, for all my supposed celebration, I still couldn't ingest the true value of my discovery:

Books make the world bigger.

CHAPTER 20

REVENGE HURTS ONLY YOU

I'm not sure if this world lets you have a spring in your step, but the next morning I sure felt like it did. Moseying down for another sure-to-be successful mining adventure, I couldn't have been in a better mood. Armed with repaired tools and weapons and a pack full of all kinds of food, I felt ready for anything. What I wasn't ready for was an age-old enemy waiting to sabotage my new, seemingly invincible winning streak.

Of all the foes waiting below, the one I really should have been ready for was me.

Heading back into the mine complex, I found my usual welcoming committee of zombies, skeletons, and even a couple of creepers. I took them out, pocketed their remains, and went off down a dark, unexplored tunnel.

This one was broken by a section of natural cave that was lit by a column of lava. After surrounding its impact point with cobblestone, I noticed a block of diamonds embedded in the smooth gray floor. This reminded me that I hadn't run across any natural diamonds except when nearby lava, and I made a mental note to prove that theory later on.

After collecting three glittering stones, I kept going until the natural cave returned to an oak-reinforced mineshaft. This time minecart tracks led me right to another chest, and another world-expanding jackpot.

I didn't find one book; I found three! And they were all about redstone, which turned out to be its actual official name. This entire time I'd seen the crimson mineral as next-to-useless, and now I was learning that it might just be the most useful material in this world. The dim redstone torch I'd thought inferior to a brighter coal version was actually a source of energy, and that energy could be transmitted by a trail of redstone dust.

And that was just the first book. Skipping to the other two, I saw that redstone was an essential building material in machines.

Yes, machines! Finally, after going from the Stone Age to the Iron Age, here was the Industrial Revolution! And if I'd just been a little more patient, taking the books home instead of skimming the pages right then and there, everything probably would've been fine.

But I didn't.

"Sssp!"

I knew that hiss. I'd heard it far too many times.

"Sssp!"

Head up, Flash ready, and books safely packed away, I pivoted to face the threat.

All clear. Behind me was the well-lit, empty passageway. Before me was only darkness. No cluster eyes, and yet . . .

"Sssp!"

I crept cautiously down the tunnel, placing torches as I went, still clinging to the thought that cave spiders were just smaller, bothersome pests.

At least I got the smaller part right.

It scuttled out of the darkness toward me, greenish-blue and about half the size of its surface cousin. I swung my sword, missed, and expected nothing more than the usual, if not milder, spider bite.

Wrong!

Pain flooded my system with the burning, choking, familiar sting of poison. I staggered back, head swimming, limbs aching, Flash flailing wildly at the turquoise snapper. Knocking it back with my shield, I lunged forward with a killing blow.

Still smarting from the venom, I reached for a milk bucket and the new, painful realization that size doesn't matter. Only then did I notice that the hissing hadn't stopped. *Well now*, I thought nervously, *at least the others won't surprise me this time!*

Wrong again.

I headed down the passageway, ready to repel any threats in front of me. Only they weren't in front of me; they were below. I passed a hole in the wooden floor, just one open block. In my anxious distraction, I figured that spiders couldn't squeeze through such a teeny opening. I didn't factor in this new, small variety. Panic drowns thought.

I'd already passed the hole when I was jumped from behind. Toxins coursing through my veins, I spun in time to catch the second of two arachnids. It reeled as its partner struck, injecting another murderous dose. Parry, slash, smoke! Another antidote of milk and more loaves of healing bread. I peered down the hole, saw nothing, and guessed—hoped, really—that there couldn't possibly be more of them down there.

Let me just say, for the record, that my thoughts hadn't been this frazzled in a long time. I'd been so used to winning, so used to things going my way, that when confronted by a genuine challenge, my mental recovery time was way out of whack.

That's why I didn't retreat the moment I jumped through the hole and saw that the entire shaft before me was filled, from top to bottom, with webs.

Of all the ironies . . . spider silk had once been so rare and precious that I'd risked my life to get it. Now I'd risk my life to get past it, to get to the spawner I saw at the end of the hallway.

At least I wasn't stupid enough to try walking through the webs, but trying to hack them away was just as idiotic. I'd barely sliced through four of the stretched, creepy cubes when I saw another spider gliding effortlessly forward, as if the sticky threads didn't exist.

I swung and struck silk. It leapt. I winced. The bite didn't poison me, but the impact knocked me right up into a web.

I was stuck!

Legs kicking, feet dangling. Slowly dipping toward the ground.

Another pounce, a second bite. This time the fangs sank deep. I screamed from the noxious fluid, cutting furiously at the entangling net. My feet hit the floor just as the first spider sprang, and landed right on Flash's diamond blade.

I retreated from the web wall just long enough to take my last drink of anti-venom milk. Before I could reach for healing food, another pair of spiders attacked. This time I was ready. I hit one, then the other, knocking them back like this was a crazy solo game of racquetball. Again they charged; again I struck. Shield and sword, bash and slash.

As the second one evaporated, I glimpsed another pair poofing up from the distant spawner. "I'll be back!" I shouted, fury roiling up within me. "I'll be back and you'll be dead! You'll all be dead!"

Running all the way home should have given me the chance to clear my head. It didn't. It should have calmed me just long enough to realize that I needed to repair my battered armor, fix my cracked sword, get a decent night's rest, and come up with a rational, reasonable plan.

It didn't. I just grabbed some more food, extra feathers for arrows, and rushed right back out to do battle. Stopping to milk Moo should have given me one last chance for sanity, but of course, it didn't.

I can only imagine what my four-legged lifeline might have said if she'd been human, what her sharp, multiple "moos" might have meant.

"Please don't do this. Don't go back there without thinking! Consider the mistakes you've made, the lessons you've learned, all the times you've almost died! Please just take a moment, take a deep breath, and don't throw away everything because you want—"

Revenge.

That's why I didn't listen to her, to my subconscious thoughts. Those creatures had reintroduced me to fear. They'd reminded me what it felt like to be helpless and weak and scared down to my DNA.

Fear made me hate, and hate made me blind. The lesson was clear, obvious, and ignored: Revenge hurts only me.

I would learn it the hard way soon enough.

I sprinted down into the depths, right back into the tunnel

where I'd started. After sealing the hole in the floor that I'd originally jumped through, I tried picking out a new one just above
the spawner itself. I planned, if you could call it that, to smash
the cage from above before any new arachnids got to me.

The plan failed. As soon as the hole opened, a spider jumped
up into my face. Recoiling from the venom, I gave the creature
several rapid hacks. *It's not failure that matters but how you recover, right?*

I recovered miserably.

Sealing the hole, then gulping milk, I groped for a rash and
reckless Plan B. Would you have tried to mine a staircase down
the wall next to the spawner? Would you have believed, or
wanted to believe, that somehow there weren't any webs on the
other side of the hall? Of course not. That's what a brain is for.

But I did, and within seconds of knocking out the final
blocks, a trio of poisonous hissers pounced. I honestly don't remember how I killed them all. All I can recollect is reaching for
a second dose of milk and realizing I'd only brought one.

The next minute was an excruciating race between hyper-
healing and the spider's digestive juice. I tried to stuff my face
with as much food as my stomach would allow, praying that I
could self-repair before the acid devoured me from within.

Veins cooling, muscles repairing, I heard another, high-
pitched rasp. Two more arthropods were scampering at me
through their protective webs, cutting me off from the staircase.

Withdraw. Retire. Run!

I beat it down the dark, unexplored tunnel. No time for torches. No thought of direction. I just ran until the hissing finally faded.

Time to rest and regroup.

I could see now that the mineshaft had given way to a rough, natural cave. Just as I placed a torch, two arrows struck me in the back.

I turned to see another cobblestone spawning chamber right behind me, with a pair of skeletons emerging from its exit. I swung, connected, and heard the SNAP of the glimmering blade shatter.

Flash had been a magnificent weapon, but I hadn't repaired its wounds. I'd seen how all the combat, and especially web chopping, had taken such a horrid toll on its fractured, chipping form. I'd seen it but I didn't do anything about it. And because I didn't take care of Flash, it couldn't take care of me.

Curses echoing in the darkness, I searched my pack and belt. No axe. No backup sword. Nothing but two arrows for my bow. I had gaggles of spare feathers, but I'd forgotten to bring any flint.

Two more skeletons emerged. Four arrows clunked off my shield. Back into the tunnel and the pitch-black unknown. I fled blindly, whistling arrows in pursuit.

Running, panting, murky stone racing past me on all sides.

Finally, silence.

My thoughts were a jumble. *Eat. Heal. Food gone. Alone in the dark.*

Lost!

Running from tunnel to tunnel, I stuck torches everywhere. *How do I get back? Where am I going?*

Panic drowns thought.

"Help," I whimpered softly, tracing and retracing the same nondescript steps. "Please, somebody! Anybody! Please, help me!"

I was right back where I had started, right back in that ocean, scared and alone and wishing for someone else to find me.

And someone did, but not in the way I wanted.

"Gruuuh!"

I heard the moan the moment I turned the corner. A low-ceiling cave, another spawning chamber. *Zombies! So many approaching zombies!*

I dashed away down another new tunnel and once again ended up blundering through the dark.

"Gruuuh!"

Zombies never give up. Slow, steady. They never let you go.

Groans bounced off the walls. They were just a few steps behind me.

Something blinked off to my right: a creeper! I twisted for a quick bow shot.

Thunk! Square in the mottled face.

Not enough. The crackling of a fuse. One more shot and—

"Squeak!" A bat, flying right between us, took the hit.

Boom!

I was blasted back, my thrashed chest plate disintegrating from my burned body.

I landed hard, splashing into shallow water that carried me farther into the gloom. "Grrr . . ." They were still behind me, dim growling shapes against the faint glow of distant torches.

I ran through the water and crashed into solid rock. I looked right and left but couldn't see anything. Nowhere to run, no way to fight.

The smell of rotting flesh was overpowering. Rotting flesh and . . . earth!

Cubes of dirt in the wall, reminding me of the first night. Buried and safe!

Grabbing the loose cobblestones from my pack, I threw up a wall across the rough opening of the tunnel. I worked furiously, automatically, and as a zombie came into view, I slammed the last block into place.

CHAPTER 21

KNOWLEDGE, LIKE A SEED, NEEDS THE RIGHT TIME TO BLOOM

"How do I survive?" I asked the darkness. "What's my next move?"

Trapped, cornered, alone.

Well, almost.

"Guhhh," moaned the zombie on the other side of the wall, completing my déjà vu.

"Same as it ever was," I answered. "Just like my first night."

And then something happened that I never would have predicted: I smiled.

"My first night," I repeated, setting down a comforting torch, "and look what I had then compared to what I have now."

"Guhhh," snarled the ghoul. Two actually, as I could hear a second one approaching.

"No, not in my pack," I laughed, wishing I could point to my head. "Up here! All those priceless lessons in my brain, all that hard-won experience. You can't take that away. Nobody can. This isn't the same as my first night because I'm not the same person!"

"Guhhh," growled the monsters.

"We'll talk later," I said, turning my back on the wall. "I gotta get to work."

I took a deep breath and visualized the Way of the Cube: Plan, Prepare, Prioritize, Practice, Patience, Persevere.

Right now I had to prioritize my needs, and need number one was food. The spider's sting had ripped every last calorie out of me. My head swam, my breath stank, and those tiny, telling shivers were back. Starvation.

Been a long time, I thought, searching my belt and pack.

All I had was one brown mushroom, totally inedible without its red and white partner.

The rest of my inventory consisted of two dozen blocks of birch, twenty blocks of oak that I'd hacked out of the mineshaft supports, three empty metal buckets, one bucket of water, a worn shovel, a worn bow, a worn pickaxe, a ton of cobblestone, some gunpowder, some redstone, three books on redstone, a bundle of feathers, and enough spider silk to make an army of fishing poles.

"Too bad there aren't any oceans nearby," I muttered. But right on the heels of those defeatist words came an exultant "There is!"

Like a crack of lightning, the memory of the food book's passage flashed across my mind. "Any body of water," it had read. *Any* body! That lifesaving fact then merged with my firsthand experience with irrigation. Remember way back when I bored you to death with my story of pouring water in a ditch? Remember when I said how important it would be later on? Well, later on was now.

"Water makes water!" I called to the zombies outside. "All I need now's a second cube."

"Uhhh," they responded, reminding me that there was more water . . . right out there with them.

Of course I'm talking about the little underground stream I'd fallen into after almost being blown up. I thought I'd seen the source: a single cube spring in the wall just a few paces from this cave. But how to get there?

I thought about the two end-around tunneling tactics I'd tried before. Both had been risky, and neither had ended well.

But now, with water so close . . .

"With great risks come great rewards!" I called to my undead jailors, and hoisted my nearly broken pickaxe.

I began hammering away, estimating where the water's source was. "And here we . . ."

I turned sharply to the left. The block fell. No water, just a couple of rotting hands.

I yelped as one green fist punched me square in the honker.

"Thanks," I said, sealing up the hole. I don't think zombies can laugh, but those moans sure sounded cheery. Clearly they were following me on the other side of the tunnel. If I made another mistake, broke through and took more damage I couldn't heal from . . .

SNAP. The iron tool broke in my hands.

"No problem!" I called to the zombies, and whipped up first a crafting table, then a stone-tipped pickaxe. "Perseverance!" Turns out I only had one more block to go. Pick, pick, pick, then WHOOSH! Underground water!

Capturing it in an empty milk pail, I dug out a large basin in the center of the cave.

Jumping inside, I poured the two water cubes against two of the corners. As they flowed together, a third cube formed between them. I repeated the process again and again and again until soon I was climbing out of a fully-filled pool.

"And here we go," I said, crafting a new fishing pole.

"Uggghhh," taunted one of the zombies.

"You're right," I hollered back. "No reason to think any body of water also means one I made. But," I said, stepping back to cast out, "you should never assume anything."

Nothing. Not even bubbles on the surface.

"Patience," I warned my ghoul captors. "You'll see, I just need to be pa—"

And there it was! That little, lifesaving V of bubbles.

"C'mon," I coaxed, waiting for the V to zigzag toward my hook. My bobber sank, the pole yanked, and an impossible salmon came flying up into my belt, along with a new lesson. Knowledge, like a seed, needs the right time to bloom.

As the day, or night, or whatever it was, wore on, my belt pouches overflowed with fish. My newly-crafted furnace filled the cave with delicious smells, and eventually the zombies, unlike my stomach, were the only things left growling.

Oh, and just in case you're wondering, yes, it did bother me having to kill to live, but if you go back a few chapters, you'll see, and I quote, if "pushed to the brink of starvation with no other choices left." Compromising an ideal in order to save it. Vegetarian to temporary pescatarian. Okay? We cool?

Moving on to my next priority: making a bed. Nothing clears the mind like a good night's sleep.

Trying to recall what I'd read about crafting wool blocks from webs, I began setting the rest of my spider twine on the crafting table. Crazy as it sounds, they combined into several soft, wooly cubes. Three wood planks later, I had a bed no different than any I'd made before. Even the blanket and pillow felt as smooth and soft as sheep's wool.

"It's going to be okay," I told myself, as the walls of my cave faded to black. "Tomorrow, I'm gettin' outta here."

But tomorrow, as they say, was *not* just a day away. The next morning, I realized that trying to make a hasty run for it would probably put me in the same position that I was in now, if not worse.

I was totally unarmed, with half my body unarmored. No milk meant I'd need ten times as much food to counter spider poison, and, let's not forget, I had no idea where I was going.

As badly as I wanted to escape the stuffy, cramped confines of my cave, I needed to repair, restock, and rethink my overall exit strategy. Like it or not, this underground chamber was going to be home for a while.

I spent two full days catching a school of fish. Once that priority was checked, I turned to the next on the list: armor and weapons.

Using the last of my worn shovel to dig out a dirt section of the wall, I found a cache of three iron cubes. *Just the start*, I thought optimistically, and picking them out, I broke through to another cave.

"Whoa," I said, backing up quickly. No mobs came through and no sounds warned of their presence. Peeking in, all I could see were a few small red and white caps dotting the floor. Mushrooms.

"Figures," I said sourly. "All that time catching fish and I could have been collecting food right here."

But then again, I reminded myself, *learning to make a fishing hole anywhere means you'll never ever starve again.*

Problems force progress.

Long story short, I'm not a fan of mushroom stew. Too creamy and bland. But, at least I didn't have to kill to eat anymore. See, I care!

And—this is a big ol' AND—mushrooms grow by themselves. Just place one on the stone floor with dim light and it'll make more of itself. So they not only cleared my conscience, they cleared my calendar, freeing me up to go mining.

And mine I did. By the ninth or tenth day, I had found enough iron and coal to forge tools, weapons, and a whole new suit of armor.

It was time to get home, but how? I still didn't know where I was going, and the path I'd taken before was way too dangerous.

I thought about maybe tunneling straight, spiral staircase style. Hopefully, I'd break through onto my island, maybe right by Moo and the sheep.

I didn't. I must have been close though, maybe at the foot of one of the slopes, because eventually I broke through to a column of sand. *The beach!* I thought happily, and shoveled the tan block away, and the one that fell in after that, and the one that fell in after that, on and on and on until seawater eventually washed me right back down into my cave.

Plan B, I thought, gloomily sealing up the breach. Plan B meant trying to tunnel far enough around the mob-infested passages to hopefully break through into another open shaft.

It didn't go exactly as planned. On the first try I broke through into an open lava cave, its walls lined with gold and diamonds. "You can't help me now," I sneered at the treasure, and tunneled in another direction. This time I finally got what I was looking for: a silent, clear shaft with no mobs anywhere in sight. Even better, the lack of torches told me I'd never been down this way.

"Home," I breathed, already tasting the sea air. Taking one step into the passageway though, I turned to my left and saw another minecart.

Throwing open the lid, I found some iron ingots, some gunpowder, a loaf of very welcome bread, and most important, another book entitled *Navigation*.

At that moment, I felt like the luckiest person ever.

"Guhhh . . ."

A zombie lurched around the corner, cracking its fist on my face. I staggered back a half step, took the second blow square on my new shield, then laid in with a series of chops from my new iron sword. Filling the hall with death smoke filled my heart with pride. I was back. I was ready. I was . . .

. . . facing three more coming down the hall.

Must be near the spawner, I thought, blocking up the tunnel behind me. Plan B was dead. Time for Plan C, which I didn't have yet. Hopefully this new book on navigation would help with that.

And it did!

There were four items described in the manual: a map, a compass, signposts, and, of all things, a journal. I couldn't make the map because I needed sugarcane for paper, and I couldn't make the journal for the same reason. The signposts were easy though, since they were just made of wood, and the compass only needed iron and redstone.

Unlike the compasses of my world, the needle didn't point north. Instead the book said it always faced my "original spawning point." Not immediately helpful, when you consider that was the bottom of the ocean, but since it always faced the same direction, I could use that consistency to keep me from getting turned around.

Laying the compass ingredients on the crafting table reminded me of how useless redstone had originally been, which, in turn, reminded me that I still had the three redstone books in my pack.

I hadn't looked at them since the initial discovery, and even then, I'd only skimmed them. *Did I miss anything useful?* I wondered, now carefully re-reading each page.

And indeed I had, rushing to take in all the fancy, cool machinery, skipping whole passages that didn't grab my attention right away.

Details make the difference.

Book three, page five, one simple sentence: "Redstone Torches can be used as the detonation source for TNT."

TNT!?

The gunpowder! *That's* what it was for!

TNT, which stands for . . . well, I don't know, but I sure knew what it did!

The book didn't say anything else about TNT, and I didn't need to know.

And you don't need to know everything I did in the underground month that followed. That's how long I spent down there, learning to craft TNT from gunpowder and sand, then testing it in the water-cooled lava cave I'd found. You don't need to know about the diamonds I mined for a new sword and armor, or the flint I gathered for more arrows, or how I used those arrows on silent raids, sneaking out of my cave to snipe at creepers for their gunpowder. Last but not least, you don't need to hear every detail about the masses of machines I learned how to build and test and weave into my elaborate, meticulous plan. All you need to know is one word.

I was still going to escape, but not before destroying every spawner and random mob I could find. This wasn't hotheaded revenge anymore. This was cold calculation. This would finally make my island, above and below, completely safe. This was the one word you need to know, the word from my world that isn't nice but is sometimes necessary. I was now going to bring that word to this world.

I was going to war.

CHAPTER 22

THE END AND THE BEGINNING

I moved silently, or at least as silently as this world would let me. Pat-pat-pat went my armored feet, with the occasional POP of a placed signpost. Following the compass needle, I headed in what I thought was the direction of the spiders' hall.

"Sssp!"

"And so it begins," I whispered, rounding the corner into the same passageway where I'd been defeated, the one right above the web spinners. Mindful of being ambushed, I quickly sealed up both ends of the shaft with cobblestone and wooden doors.

Next I blocked up the staircase I'd made down to the lower hall. Finally, I snuck right up to that hole in the floor and removed the blocking stone.

Two crimson clusters sparkled up at me, ready to spring. "Bath time," I said, and poured a bucket of lava down the hole. In seconds, the liquid fire burned through my attackers, their webs, and the caged spawn flame beneath them.

I didn't gloat. I didn't even react. I just scooped up the molten cube, watched the residual lava dissipate, and prepared for more arachnid stragglers. None came. I'd won my first tactical engagement swiftly, silently, and without so much as a scratch.

Moving on to the skeletons' spawning chamber, I heard a chorus of clicks well before any of them came into view. Four outside, and no doubt more within. They saw me; I saw them. Their bows went up, but my shield didn't. It was worth taking a few arrows in order to set up my new wonder weapons.

They were called dispensers, and the book described them as a kind of vending machine. They were designed to hold a lot of items, spitting one out when triggered. I guess they were supposed to be labor-saving conveniences, but it was easy to see them as weaponry.

No tools or torches for these dispensers, just loads of deadly arrows. I placed a trip wire of spider silk and iron hooks—thank you, redstone books!—in a line between the dispensers and the skeletons, and stood back to watch the oncoming archers.

"Dispense with this," I said, laughing at my joke as the relentless shafts hammered those boneheads like the machine guns of my world. The barrage didn't kill them right away. It didn't have to. My point was to delay and distract. While the skeletons absorbed an overdose of their own medicine, I tunneled around them and into the back wall of the spawning chamber.

I broke through into the darkened room just in time to see a fresh bonebag emerge from the caged flame.

"Say good night, hotshot," I said with a chuckle, diamond blade flashing.

After smashing the spawning cage, I poked my head through the doorway to watch my dispensers claim their last victim.

I made sure to go back the way I came, because, like fire, booby traps have no loyalty, then set to work disassembling them. The war was far from over, and both arrows and dispensers still had a lot of work to do.

My next trap involved a dispenser and a small, previously unused item called a flint and steel. It was a C-shaped piece of iron and a flint chip that, when struck together, caused a small, temporary blaze. I'd accidentally made one a while back, but couldn't think of a use.

I did now.

When placed in a dispenser and then set next to a pressure plate, it acted as a kind of rearguard land mine. Remember, in addition to spawners, there were still random patches of darkness that created the occasional mob.

Just as I was setting my first trap, the groan of a zombie filled the passageway. I looked up to see the undead attacker lurching from out of the gloom. I backed up a few steps, but not so far that I risked losing contact. The zombie came on, slow and dumb and completely unaware of the danger.

"Don't stop," I encouraged. "Come and get it."

It stepped on the pressure plate, which activated the dispenser, which sparked the flint striker, which set the green ghoul ablaze. Burning like a torch, it growled and gurgled toward me.

"Burn, baby, burn!" I chanted, retreating just as quickly as it advanced. After a few seconds I saw that fire wouldn't finish the ghoul. It weakened it, though. I only needed one strong chop.

Good enough, I thought, placing more striker mines in the passageway behind me. And they did their job splendidly. I could hear the cries of burning ghouls echoing through the tunnels. "I'll put all of you out of your misery soon enough," I called, focusing on my next booby trap.

What this one lacked in imagination, it more than made up for in lethality. A pressure plate, a trapdoor, and a hole filled with lava.

"Hey, Blasty," I shouted to a nearby creeper. "Over here!"

Weirdly, the living bomb turned in the other direction. "No, doofus!" I shouted, and raised my bow. "Here!"

I shot the creeper in the back, hoping, if you can believe it, for a less than lethal kill. The green, silent column turned back, locked on me, and slowly glided forward.

"Right!" I said, backing up past its invisible detonation range. "Here's your target!"

The creeper swept over the pressure plate, then dropped through the trapdoor. Bobbing and burning, it silently surrendered to its fate.

"Shame," I said, watching my foe disintegrate. "I could have used the gunpowder."

I found my way back to the main cavern, specifically to a shaft that opened right up above a lava pond. Just as I was setting up my new horror show, I heard a growing cackle. A jackpot of two witches came around the corner, bottles of who-knows-what in their hands.

"Perfect!" I called to the approaching villains. "You, of all mobs, deserve what's coming."

With the flick of a lever, I sent a minecart racing down a powered rail. This new combination of wood, gold, and, of course, redstone, sent the automated missile crashing into the oncoming witches.

Cackling maniacally, they toppled right off the cliff, and into the liquid fire. "Who's laughing now?" I shouted, realizing a second later that, in fact, they still were. "Yeah, well . . . I still get the last laugh."

I hopped into a minecart, a stacked collection of tracks in my hand. Leaning forward, just like in a boat, I found I was able to make the cart move on its own. Placing new tracks in front of me, and connecting them to existing rail lines allowed me to zip along the mineshafts like a racecar.

If I hadn't been at war, the ride probably would have been fun.

Soon enough, I thought, racing through endless tunnels. *Once this whole maze is cleared, I'll build a roller coaster down here. Wouldn't that be cool!*

Laying track as I went, and steering on a specific course, I checked off my list of victories. *Spiders: gone. Skeletons: gone. Random patches of darkness: lit. Random passages: booby-trapped.*

Just one more, I thought excitedly. *One more spawner, and then I've won!*

Coming to rest at the base of the zombies' spawning chamber, I leapt out of the cart and ran like a maniac for the door.

"Guhhh," growled a ghoul, poking its head out of the entrance.

"Stay!" I commanded, bashing it back inside with my shield. I wanted it trapped, not dead. Before it could regroup for another strike, I placed two glass blocks in the opening.

Glass? Yep, glass. I not only used it to seal up the doorway, but I also replaced the entire cobblestone wall with clear cubes. I had something very special planned for my slouching friends.

After finishing the first glass wall, I built a second, identical barrier one block behind it, and then filled in the space between them with water.

Why water, you ask? Because it was the only substance that could absorb the blast of TNT.

I hit upon the idea from that first explosive creeper. Remember how it had blown a hole in the bank of the lagoon? Well, I realized that the blast had only hurt the bank itself, while the shallow, underwater blocks were unscathed.

I thought I was being so careful. I'd even tested the water-wall theory in the cooled lava cave. And it had worked.

After filling this water wall, I placed stone steps up to the top of the spawning chamber's ceiling, hollowed out a space above the roof, and filled the space with charges.

I thought I was being so careful.

Running a fuse of redstone dust all the way back to the bottom, I armed the last step with a simple wooden button. How poetically fitting that this button was the first item I'd ever crafted. Things were really coming full circle.

"You were my first threat," I sneered at the zombies, "and now you'll be the last."

A dim hidden memory took shape as I leaned in to push the button, some kind of expression about another button and another great explosion. Strangely enough, the image of a mushroom cloud crystalized in my mind.

"Bing, bang, boom," I said and pressed the small wooden square.

And then the world ended.

Or at least that's what it felt like as the earsplitting concussion blew up the room, the zombies, and the torches that lit my "victory."

"Yeeehaw," I started to yell, but was suddenly smothered in a deluge of water.

The top level of the glass wall must have shattered, I thought, and backed up to get away.

Only I couldn't back up. Something was blocking my escape. I turned to see gravel, an entire wall of the stuff, had fallen in behind me.

I looked up to see how far the barrier reached, and saw where the water was really coming from. My heart froze. I'd made a deadly mistake. I'd had no way of knowing how close the ocean floor was to me. I'd just assumed it was a mountain of rock.

Never assume anything.

The blast had not only ripped that floor wide open, but had also released a massive gravel deposit behind me.

Trapped. Drowning. There was no place to go but up!

So far.

So slow.

Cold. Dark.

CRACK!

Shooting pains through air-starved muscles.

Closer, but still so far away. My body ached, my lungs burned.

Swim!

CRACK!

Mouth open in a choked scream.

Just like before. The beginning and the end.

CRACK!

I reached for the glow, grabbing for breath, for life.

CRACK!

The end is the beginning!

CRACK!

I understand now. I get it!

EPILOGUE

"I understand now," was what I coughed to Moo. Half dead, splashing to the surface, I pulled myself painfully to shore at the feet of my loyal friend. "I understand everything," I repeated, in answer to her knowing, "about time" moo. Gulping down breaths, I limped sluggishly toward her.

"It's all coming together," I told her, the two of us walking into the woods. "When I was down there, drowning in the deep, I kept thinking about how everything had come full circle, about endings and beginnings and how they're one and the same."

By this point we'd made it over to where the sheep family was grazing. "Everybody, gather round," I announced. "I've got something important to say." Of course they didn't listen, but did it stop me talking?

"Keep going," I began. "That was the first lesson I learned here, and now it'll be the last." I took a moment to let my words sink in. "I have to accept that I'm at the end of one adventure and at the beginning of another. I've got to keep going. I've got to leave the island."

Before they could say anything, before they could pretend to not care by turning away to eat, I added, "No, no, hear me out. Like I said, I understand now. In fact, I've understood for quite a while. It's that gnawing feeling I've had since finishing the second house. It's why I've been acting so crazy since then. I didn't want to admit the scary truth."

"Which is?" mooed Moo.

"Which is," I answered, "that after working so hard to create a safe space to answer the really big questions, I realized that the answers to those questions can't be found in a safe space."

I gestured out to the horizon. "They're out there in the unknown."

"Baa," asked Rainy, as the sheep family all looked at me.

"Good question. Hopefully there's more land, more people. Hopefully I'll be able to find my way home."

Moo let out a soft, sad "moo." And that's when my tears came.

"No, you're right," I said through the lump in my throat.

"*This* is my home, too, and I'll carry its memories in my heart, because even if I don't find the answers I'm searching for, it's the searching that really matters."

There it was, the ultimate lesson of this world.

"I struggled so hard for a goal, without realizing that the goal is the struggle. It's what makes me stronger, smarter, and better. Growth doesn't come from a comfort zone, but from leaving it."

A week later I had packed up everything I needed for a long voyage. Food, tools, a compass, and a yet-to-be-filled map. I made sure the garden was well-tended, and that the house would be ready to accept a new visitor.

That visitor, as you well know, is you. I hope you find my house comfortable, and if you want to build a basement music studio, I've left you the book, along with all the other manuals, in my bedroom. This book that you're reading was the last item in the last manual I found, a combination of sugar-paper, leather from Moo's late partner, and ink from the squid I killed way back but couldn't find a use for. Figures.

These will be the last words I write before walking down the hill to my boat, before saying goodbye to my beloved friends. Please treat them well. Friends keep you sane.

I don't know what's waiting beyond the horizon, but now I'm ready for a bigger world. Maybe I'll meet the authors of the books I've found. Maybe they'll be castaways like me. Maybe they've intentionally left those books to help future travelers with their journeys, the way I'm leaving this book for you.

I hope what I've learned helps you find your way. Most of all, I hope you've learned that in this world of mines and crafting, the most important thing you can craft is you.

WHAT I'VE LEARNED FROM

THE WORLD OF MINECRAFT

1. Keep going, never give up.

2. Panic drowns thought.

3. Don't assume anything.

4. Think before you act.

5. Details make the difference.

6. Just because the rules don't make sense to you doesn't mean that they don't make sense.

7. Figuring out the rules turns them from enemies into friends.

8. Be grateful for what you have.

9. It's not wisdom that counts but wisdom under pressure.

10. Too much confidence can be as dangerous as having none at all.

11. Take life in steps.

12. Friends keep you sane.

13. Conserve your resources.

14. Tantrums never help.

15. Nothing clears the mind like sleep.

16. When looking for solutions, beating yourself up isn't one of them.

17. Don't dwell on mistakes; learn from them.

18. Great risk can come with great rewards.

19. Fear can be conquered. Anxiety must be endured.

20. Courage is a full-time job.

21. When the world changes, you've got to change with it.

22. Always be aware of your surroundings.

23. There's nothing wrong with careful curiosity.

24. Take care of your environment, so it can take care of you.

25. Just because someone looks like you doesn't automatically make them a friend.

26. Just because someone *doesn't* look like you doesn't automatically make them an enemy.

27. Everything comes at a price. Especially if that price is your conscience.

28. It's not failure that matters, it's how you recover.

29. When you're trying to tell yourself something, listen.

30. Questions don't stay put; you can't just walk away from them.

31. Never put off the boring but important chores.

32. Sometimes you have to compromise an ideal in order to save it.

33. Books make the world bigger.

34. Revenge hurts only you.

35. Knowledge, like a seed, needs the right time to bloom.

36. Growth doesn't come from a comfort zone, but from leaving it.

ACKNOWLEDGMENTS

To Jack Swartz, who first introduced the Brooks family to Minecraft.

To the folks at Mojang, Lydia and Junk, for letting me play in their sandbox.

To Ed Victor, who, as always, continues to believe in me.

A BIG thank you to Sarah Peed, the Spock to my Kirk.

To my wife, my beacon, Michelle.

And finally to my mom, who, long ago, thought it would be a good idea to read a book called *Robinson Crusoe* to her son.

ABOUT THE AUTHOR

MAX BROOKS is an author, public speaker, and non-resident fellow at the Modern War Institute at West Point. His bestselling books include *The Zombie Survival Guide* and *World War Z,* which was adapted into a 2013 movie starring Brad Pitt. His graphic novels include *The Extinction Parade, G.I. Joe: Hearts & Minds,* and the #1 *New York Times* bestseller *The Harlem Hellfighters.*

maxbrooks.com
Facebook.com/AuthorMaxBrooks